JOB #:

Author Name:

Title of Book:

ISBN:9780791470664

Publisher:

Trim Size:5.5x8.5

Bulk in mm:10

Praise for *Wang in Love and Bondage*

"The translation by Zhang and Sommer is excellent. It both expresses the meaning of the original and also catches the simple, colloquial, and direct language that is Wang Xiaobo's trademark … By translating Wang's work, they have provided a service to all of us who teach modern Chinese literature. Because the Chinese original is easy to read, and because the translators have captured this simple yet profound style, the book should be a welcome addition to modern literature courses in translation."

— *Modern Chinese Language and Culture*

"Wang injects an unsavory history with irony, lifting the burden of the past and transforming it into hope for the future."

— *World Books*, PRI

"Loved and revered by college students throughout China, Wang Xiaobo's black humor and licentious satires have finally been translated into English."

— *Small Swords Magazine*

"The novellas move along at a good pace, and there's quite a bit of humour here."

— *The Complete Review*

"Hongling Zhang and Jason Sommer have done a remarkable job with their judicious choices, accurate renditions of the Chinese originals, and faithful preservation of the author's irreverent attitude toward everything in sight."

— Yunzhong Shu, author of *Buglers on the Homefront: The Wartime Practice of the Qiyue School*

Wang in Love and Bondage

Wang in Love and Bondage

Three Novellas
by Wang Xiaobo

Translated and with an Introduction by
Hongling Zhang
Jason Sommer

STATE UNIVERSITY OF NEW YORK PRESS

Cover illustration by Mulele Jarvis

Published by
State University of New York Press, Albany

Printed in the United States of America

For information, contact State University of New York Press,
www.sunypress.edu

Production by Marilyn P. Semerad
Marketing by Susan M. Petrie

Library of Congress Cataloging in Publication Data

Wang, Xiaobo, 1952-
[Novels. English. Selections]
Wang in love and bondage : three novellas by Wang Xiaobo / Xiaobo Wang ; translated and with an Introduction by Hongling Zhang, Jason Sommer.
p. cm.
Includes bibliographical references and index.
ISBN-13: 978-0-7914-7065-7 (hbk. : alk. paper) 1. Wang, Xiaobo, 1952—Translations into English. I. Zhang, Hongling. II. Sommer, Jason. III. Title.

PL2919.H8218A25 2007
891.53'52—dc22

2006013801

10 9 8 7 6 5 4 3 2 1

CONTENTS

INTRODUCTION

On April 11, 1997, in his suburban Beijing apartment, Wang Xiaobo died of a sudden heart attack. That May he would have celebrated his forty-fifth birthday and the debut of a three-volume collection of his fiction, which had been rejected in various forms by more than twenty publishers. His death shocked his friends in addition to a growing readership, who had begun to know his name through his satiric essays, models of the revived *zawen* genre, an important vehicle in twentieth-century China for making social commentary and initiating intellectual trends. More than a hundred newspapers and magazines throughout the country reported the loss of an original thinker and literary pioneer and noted the posthumous publication of his novellas. Within months his fame had spread throughout China.

Since then nearly all his work has been published and kept in print. His trilogy, comprising two novella collections and a novel—*The Golden Age*, *The Silver Age*, and *The Bronze Age*—sold eighty thousand copies in its first printing and was selected as one of the ten most influential books of 1997 in China. Two *zawen* collections, *My Spiritual Home* and *The Silent Majority*, published that same year, remain best sellers. To this day the so-called Wang Xiaobo fever hasn't cooled any. He has become a cult figure among university students and a cultural phenomenon at the turn of the new century.

The popularity of his fiction in particular had been slow in coming, though, and the interest he generated on university campuses as a novelist did not mean in China acceptance by the literary establishment, which was located elsewhere. Many of the most important figures in Chinese letters in the nineties, members of the writers' union, for example, were neither university trained, nor university based. A public—including Wang's contemporary creative writers—might have thought itself well prepared for the fiction by the *zawen*, which tackled almost all issues of significance to the intelligentsia: the collective hysteria in the Cultural Revolution and its variations in the new era, the fate of Chinese intellectuals in the twentieth century and the call for a rational and scientific spirit, the save-the-world complex and fanatical nationalism, the moral and cultural conservatism in China and the cultural relativism in the West, feminism, homosexuality, and environmental protection. However, many who read the fiction because of his *zawen* were disappointed. While they recognized the quirky logic and ironic wit that were the hallmarks of his *zawen*, they felt confused by the ambiguity of the subject matter of his fiction, the frank and unsentimental approach to sexuality, and his innovative style. The literary establishment simply ignored his fiction. Positive critical reception tended to come from scholars who were not necessarily specialists in literature, with the notable exception of Professor Ai Xiaoming of Zhongshan University, who first recognized Wang's avant-garde talent and has written extensively about him. We rely here on *The Romantic Knight*, a collection of materials about Wang, which Ai edited with Wang's widow, Li Yinhe. Beyond Ai Xiaoming and several others, mainstream creative writers and literary critics maintain a relative silence to the present time.

Despite the initial controversy and pockets of continuing indifference, Wang Xiaobo's fame as a novelist has grown steadily over the last nine years, as has the evidence of his influence in literary and cultural circles. On the fifth anniversary of Wang's death in 2002, a group of his admirers, mostly young people, published a collection of fiction in tribute to him that imitates his style, titled *The Running Dogs at Wang Xiaobo's Door.* The internationally renowned director Zhang Yuan collaborated with Wang to make the film *East Palace, West Palace* from Wang's story "Sentiments Like Water," written for the film. (Since story and screenplay were written almost simultaneously, and the film is responsible for what awareness Westerners may have of Wang, we use the film title for the novella included in this book.) Zhang is considering adapting "The Golden Age," another of the stories in this collection, for the screen, as well.

On April 11, 2005, the eighth anniversary of his death, an exhibition celebrating his life and writing was held in Lu Xun Museum, which marks the official recognition of Wang Xiaobo as one of the major literary figures of twentieth-century China.

The museum exhibition, among the other commemorations and publications, not only serves notice of the end of outsider status, but also draws attention to the facts of Wang Xiaobo's life that illuminate that status. The personal background of any writer is an account of influences, and Wang's family history certainly contains elements of obvious significance for his fiction. His father, Wang Fang Ming, was a famous logician. His older brother, Wang Xiaoping, followed his father, studying under the founder of Mathematical and Symbolic Logic in China, Shen Youding, and received his PhD in philosophy in 1988 from Tulane University. (Wang Xiaobo often uses the language of logic for parody.) Wang was the fourth eldest of five children, and would have been, in the traditional methods of ranking sons, an "Er," or number two son, like so many of his fictional protagonists. Wang was born in 1952, the year his father was labeled an alien-class element and purged from the Communist Party. His mother named him Xiaobo—small wave—in hopes that the political tide would be just that. The turning was not to come until 1979. He writes about his family's political danger in *The Silent Majority*, so titled because the situation of his family, their silencing and their peril, was so common among members of his generation.

In Wang Xiaobo's case, through his family, that common fate had some compensations. Growing up, he had the privilege of reading the world's classic literature in translation while others had to recite Chairman Mao's little red book. In his famous essay "My Spiritual Home," he reminisces about how, in his childhood, he and his brother often got into trouble by stealing books from their father's locked bookcases. Among the volumes under lock and key were Ovid's *Metamorphoses*, Shakespeare's plays, and even Boccaccio's *Decameron*. This reading may well have helped keep his judgment intact even during the most absurd period in modern China. One telling detail in his familiarity with the Western tradition is his particular fondness for Mark Twain.

Like most of his contemporaries, Wang was sent down to the countryside to accept "peasants' reeducation" and went to university only after Mao's death in 1976. Wang studied in the

United States from 1984 to 1988, earning an MA in comparative literature from the University of Pittsburgh. He married the noted sociologist Li Yinhe in 1980. Their collaboration in the groundbreaking work, *Their World: A Study of the Male Homosexual Community in China*, supplied the basis for Wang's "East Palace, West Palace." Li Yinhe also wrote extensively about Foucault and sexuality. In 2004, she drafted a proposal on same-sex marriage and tried unsuccessfully to get the National People's Congress to pass it. Wang taught at university after his return in 1988 and then resigned to become one of the few freelance writers in China until his death.

Most of Wang Xiaobo's protagonists bear the same name, Wang Er, literally Wang Number Two. They are either city students who were sent down to the countryside for rustication during the Cultural Revolution and then returned to the city to work various factory jobs (*The Golden Age*), or artists of various sorts at various times. One lives in a dysfunctional future and needs a license to practice painting ("2015" in *The Silver Age*); another lives in the ancient Tang dynasty ("Hongfu Elopes at Midnight" in *The Iron Age*). These multiple Wang Ers, when faced with a nightmarish Orwellian world, find no traditional system sufficient to cope with reality. Both worldly Confucianism and reclusive Taoism fall short. As in Orwell's *1984*, in Wang's fictional world sex becomes an expression of rebellion against oppressive authority and of the cost of that rebellion for the individual.

These two subjects, power and sexuality, emerge as the most notable themes in Wang's fiction. It might be natural for us to assume that one—power—would be clearly dominant. Wang makes it hard to tell what is in the ascendant by approaching his subject matter with lightness, even playfulness, yet the barbs directed at the current social and political order are not blunted in any way. In his award-winning novella *The Golden Age*, a young, beautiful doctor, Chen Qingyang, has a problem with sex that threatens to place her in political jeopardy. She is haunted by a baseless rumor that, in her imprisoned husband's absence, she is promiscuous—"damaged goods" as we have translated it—an accusation that could bring down the force of the authorities, could turn her into an "object of proletarian dictatorship," and put her under "the revolutionary mass's surveillance." Having committed neither the "criminal act" nor possessing the motive to do so, Chen Qingyang feels it necessary to defend her innocence, like Joseph K in *The Trial* or the Land-Surveyor K in *The Castle*. Only the bureaucratic institutions that Kafka's protagonists deal with have given place to a tacit collusion between the voyeuristic totalitarian authority and the proletarian masses. Thinking that Wang Er, like herself sent down from Beijing, might be able to understand her plight, she goes to him for help in proving her innocence. Wang Er might have offered her sympathy easily enough—he can prove logically that Chen Qingyang is not damaged goods, but he purposely disappoints her by suggesting she become real damaged goods. Soon the story of the insulted and the injured becomes the story of a woman who actively seeks to live up to her fictitious crime—one of Wang's legacies is his refusal to portray the intellectuals who suffered in the Cultural Revolution as tragic heroes.

The logic here is quirky and Kafkaesque, not because of the mysterious and unmerited accusation but rather in the charge taken on by the protagonist to live up to and substantiate the accusation. It is what Kundera points out when defining *the Kafkan* in his essay "Somewhere Behind" in *The Art of the Novel*: first the offense seeks the punishment, then the punishment seeks the offense, and finally the punishment finds the offense. Kundera further points out that the nature of the Kafkan is not tragedy, but comedy of the absurd kind, black comedy. Wang is obviously a skilled practitioner of this genre. His insight into human absurdity, his ability to provoke laughter from horror, along with his gift of handling weighty subjects in the lightest tone, not only make him a brilliant literary pioneer in China, but also put him in the company of such masters of black comedy as George Orwell, Joseph Heller, Anthony Burgess, Kurt Vonnegut, or postmodernists such as Italo Calvino, or Donald Barthelme.

Wang's stories display many of the characteristics associated with postmodern fiction: the flattened emotional affect; the narrative reflexivity—complete with interruptions by both the author and narrators; the "anti-style" resistance to eloquence, except for the purpose of deflation, and reliance on repetition of commonplace phrases; the frank, often antic, treatment of sexuality. However, the nihilism, the failure to find value in anything, charged to so much postmodern work cannot be found at the heart of Wang's writing. Rather, as some critics point out, his deconstruction of prevailing values always points in a constructive direction. One of the themes of *The Golden Age* is love, illustrated with his peculiar logic in the following:

> I still keep the duplicates of my confessions from back then. Once, I showed them to a friend who majored in English and American literature. He said they were all very good, with the charm of Victorian underground novels. As for the details I had cut out, he said it was a good idea to cut them out, because those details destroyed the unity of the story. My friend is really erudite. I was very young when I wrote the confessions and didn't have any learning (I still don't have much learning), or any idea what Victorian underground novels were. What I had in my mind was that I shouldn't be an instigator. Many people would read my confessions. If after reading them they couldn't help screwing damaged goods, that wasn't so bad; but if they learned the other thing, that would be really bad.

Readers must wonder about "the other thing" that is even worse than "screwing damaged goods." We soon learn that it is nothing other than love.

> Chen Qingyang said that by her true sin she meant the incident on Mount Qingping. She was being carried on my shoulder then, wearing the Thai skirt that bound her legs tightly together, and her hair hung down to my waist. The white cloud in the sky hurried on its journey, and there were only two of us in the midst of mountains. I had just smacked her bottom; I spanked her really hard. The burning feeling was fading. After that I cared about nothing else but continuing to climb the mountain. Chen Qingyang said that moment she felt limp all over, so she let go of herself, hanging over my shoulder. That moment she felt like a spring vine entangling a tree, or a young bird clinging to its master. She no longer cared about anything else, and at that moment she had forgotten everything. At that moment she fell in love with me, and that would never change.

Well, it *is* love that is the true sin, the thing that ultimately makes the authorities aghast, which leads us to conclude, following the trail of the irony, that what the authorities most fear, noted so clearly by the narrator, the author most values.

But of course it is not an unproblematic love represented here and elsewhere in these novellas. (We will not be giving much away, if we suggest that it does not lead to bliss for the characters in this—or any—of his stories.) In this case of Chen Qingyang and Wang Er, there are the distinct overtones, in themselves ironic surely, of the every-woman-loves-a-fascist kind of domination in the slap on the behind that is the blow that leads to love. It's worth noting, too, that generally Wang Xiaobo's women are the masterful parties in relationships. However, this moment on the mountain certainly seems to be a parody of the traditional, not to say even outmoded, dance of dominance and submission. And the play of dominance and submission is a key area of contact between Wang Xiabao's view of the personal life and the life of the nation around him.

Dominance and submission are very much in evidence in "2015," a novella from his dystopian *The Silver Age*. In this work another Wang Er, after being put into a labor camp for the reason that people find his abstract paintings "unfathomable," falls into the hands of a sadistic policewoman; "East Palace, West Palace" presents a more clearly sadomasochistic love story, with a self-consciously masochist gay writer, Ah Lan, on one side and a handsome policeman, Xiao Shi, unaware of his homosexual and sadistic tendencies, on the other. Again, the sadistic and masochistic roles of the characters intertwine with their social roles: sadist/police versus masochist/artist. As Professor Dai Jinghua of Beijing University insightfully points out, the key to Wang's work is not Freud, but Foucault. The sadomasochistic element in his work functions not as a space for rebellion, but as a metaphor for state power and the voluntary and even enthusiastic collaboration of its subjects. According to Dai, this underscoring of the collaborative nature of the mechanism of oppression subverts the role, of suffering tragic hero, in which Chinese intellectuals love to see themselves.

Outside of China, the general association between contemporary Chinese literature and suffering, particularly with the many recent portrayals of the Cultural Revolution, may be at risk of becoming automatic. Wang Xiaobo understood this. He offers in his fiction an alternative vision: stylistically innovative and wickedly funny, which ought to disrupt any stereotypes-in-the-making, if we have done his work anything like justice in our translation. And if we have done well, what we have done well was assisted greatly by a number of people. We owe special thanks to Li Yinhe for her trust and support. Professor Ai Xiaoming, of Zhong Shan University, and Wang Xiaoping, Wang Xiaobo's brother, both of whom were generous with their time and insights into the work. We profited from the guidance of professors Howard Goldblatt and Robert Hegel. Zhang Jing and Professor Michael Berry are due our gratitude for their sound advice. Lin Ling, Zhang Jie, Tom Lavallee, Jiang Yansheng, Yang Xia, and Chen Ping helped with the finer points of language. We also want to thank the two anonymous readers, provided by State University of New York Press, for their careful reading and useful commentary.

Hongling Zhang
Jason Sommer

2015

1

I've wanted to be an artist since I was a little kid. An artist wears a corduroy jacket, leaves his hair long, and squats down by the wall of a police station—Lijiakou police station had a bare brick wall, deep gray in color; my young uncle often squatted by it, blowing air into his cheeks until they puffed up. Sometimes, the corduroy jacket he wore would puff up too, like the sheepskin rafts ferrying across the Yellow River. Then he would look fatter than usual. This image left me with the impression that artists were something like sacks. The only difference between the two is that when you get tangled up with a sack, you have to move it away with your hands; when you stumble over an artist, you kick him and he will move off by himself. In my memory, positioned at the base of a gray, shining vertical plane (that's the wall) is a brown ball (brown was the color of the corduroy jacket)—that was my young uncle exactly.

I could find my young uncle at the police station. The station had a courtyard circled by a wall of whitewashed gray bricks. A red light hung in the doorway, which would only be lit after dark. Once the people there saw me, they would shout, "Ah, the great painter's nephew is here!" It felt like home. At noon, the policemen cooked noodles in the reception room by the door. The smell of the noodle soup made me feel doubly warm. I could also find my young uncle in a nearby coffee shop called the Great Earth. The inside was always pitch-black since the electricity wasn't on, but candles filled the air with the choking smell of paraffin wax. Looking at people in the coffee shop, you could only see the lower part of their face, and these faces were all dark red, like barbecued baby pigs. He often did business with people there and also often got arrested there on the charge of selling paintings without a permit. My young uncle often committed this kind of error because he was a painter but didn't have the mandatory painter's permit. After he got arrested, somebody had to bail him out. There was a block of shops near the police station, and most of them, built in the fifties, were houses with steep tile roofs. Under the two rows of small gingko trees on the sidewalk, people built fires to barbecue lamb tips on spits, which burned the leaves yellow and made it an autumn scene year-round; later all the trees died. The place he lived wasn't far from there, a one-bedroom apartment in a tall building—the building had a square box-headed look, fairly ugly, with trash-strewn hallways. Whenever you went to see him, he was never home, though that wasn't always true.

My uncle was a painter without a permit, but what made him different from others was that he was so industrious: sometimes he painted, sometimes he sold his paintings, and therefore at other times he squatted at the police station. When he painted, he would lock the door and put on soundproof earphones, so that he couldn't hear if someone knocked on his door, and he wouldn't pick up the phone either. Alone, he faced his easel like a man in a trance. Since he lived on the fourteenth floor, nobody could lean over to the window to peek inside, so nobody had ever seen him paint except a burglar. The burglar, climbing into his apartment from a balcony on the thirteenth floor, had planned on stealing something. But after he walked into my uncle's living room and got a glimpse of his painting, he was shocked. He walked over, tapped him, and said, Hey, buddy, what the hell are you up to? My uncle had gone into his painting trance, so he snarled, Don't bother me. I'm painting. The burglar crossed to the other side of the room, squatted down, and watched him for a while. Then he couldn't help walking back over to my uncle, lifting up his left earphone and saying, Hey, you can't paint like that! My uncle, fierce as a wolf, shoved him to the floor and went on with his painting. The guy squatted on the floor for a long time, waiting to discuss the craft of painting with my uncle, but he never got the chance. Finally he opened the front door and walked out, taking my uncle's camcorder and several thousand yuan along with him. However, he left a note with a solemn warning: if you keep painting like this, you'll commit errors. Though he stole things himself, he couldn't stand watching my uncle take a wrong turn. A burglar with a conscience, he was concerned with the morality of the people he robbed. My uncle said that the note was very melodramatic, what he meant was that the note moved him.

One day, some time later, my uncle ran into the burglar who stole from him in the police station; they squatted side-by-side at the foot of the wall. According to my uncle, the burglar wore a pair of corduroy loafers, full of little holes, and another feature of the gentleman was a head of unkempt hair full of wood chips. It turned out he was a worker on various construction sites. Sometimes he worked as a carpenter, and then wood chips would get in his hair; sometimes he worked as a welder, and then the sparks would burn little holes in his shoes; sometimes he worked as a burglar, and then he would get arrested and taken to the police station. My uncle thought he looked familiar, but couldn't place him. The burglar greeted him warmly, Hey, buddy, you got nabbed, too? In a daze, my uncle thought he was a fellow artist and responded vaguely. After a while the burglar jogged his memory, Hey, remember me? We met at your apartment when I was stealing things! Only then did my uncle remember him, Oh, so it's you! *Good morning*! The two of them began chatting cordially. But the more they chatted, the less cordial they became. In the end they started to fight because the burglar said that my uncle's brain was full of the dregs of colored tofu. If the policeman hadn't hit my uncle on the back of the head, my uncle would have probably strangled the burglar since he even had the nerve to point out that something was wrong with my uncle's eyes. In fact, my uncle did have an eye problem called divergent strabismus, which was why he flew into such a rage. Favoring the burglar's ideas about art, the policeman said if the burglar hadn't been such a repeat offender, he would have been lenient and released him. Later, they used money from my uncle's pocket to buy ice cream for the burglar, letting him sit in a chair eating while my uncle squatted on the floor watching. It was a very hot day. My uncle's mouth watered as he watched the burglar eat ice cream.

I often picked up my uncle from the police station, so I often met the burglar. A peasant from around Tangshan, he'd made his living doing odd jobs in Beijing for ten years. He was a good carpenter, plumber, and tiler; if he hadn't stolen, he would've been a good person, too. They say that every time he sneaked into someone's house, he would clean the whole place, fix the leaky faucet, wipe away the greasy dirt in the kitchen, and take out the garbage; then he would ransack the place, closet to cupboard. If he came across a lot of cash, he would write a letter of accusation to the public prosecutor's office, reporting the victim on suspicion of embezzlement; if he came across very little money, he would send a letter of commendation to the victim's work unit, praising the person's integrity. He also prepared many mottoes and philosophical adages on life, you take something from the house—you leave something for the house. If the family had videotapes, he would check them one by one, confiscating the obscene ones so that the owner wouldn't be corrupted. Some families had too many videotapes, but he would still watch them one by one; as a result, the owner would come home and catch him. From the police station to the neighborhood committee, everybody believed he was a good burglar and didn't want to send him to prison. But unfortunately he stole too much. Finally they had to execute him, which made the policemen in the station and the old women in the neighborhood committee all weep for him. Before the execution, the burglar made a will, donating his body to the hospital. One of my classmates attended medical school there, often seeing him in the formaldehyde trough. The guy has a big tool, my friend said. He even looks handsome in the formaldehyde trough. No one can tell that he used to be a burglar. He took a bullet in the back of his head, but you'd never know it if his body wasn't turned over. Every time they had anatomy class, the girls would fight over him.

My uncle's crime was just a misdemeanor, but it really got on people's nerves. This was because his paintings, with their riot of color, made no sense to anyone, and no one could tell what his paintings were about. Once, I saw a policeman hold up a painting and bawl at him sternly, Young fellow—stand up and tell me—what is this? If you can tell me what this means, I'll squat there instead of you! My uncle turned and looked at his own work, then squatted down again, saying, I don't know what it is either. I'd better do my own squatting. In my opinion, he'd painted something that resembled either a huge whirlpool, or a squirrel's tail. Of course, if a squirrel grew a tail like that, it would be a real freak. Because of paintings of this sort, the permit he used to have was revoked. Before revoking his permit, the department concerned tried their best to do him a favor by printing out a list that read as follows: Work 1, "Sea Horse"; Work 2, "Kangaroo"; Work 3, "Snail"; and so on. The words in quotations were the titles that the leaders supplied for the paintings. They believed that people could understand them once the titles were given. Of course, the sea horse, kangaroo, and snail in the paintings all looked strange, like they were crazy. As long as my uncle agreed to use these titles, they would let him keep his permit. But my uncle refused to use the titles; he said he didn't paint sea horses and kangaroos. The leaders said, It's OK not to paint sea horses or kangaroos, but you have to paint something. It would have been better if my uncle hadn't breathed a word, but he argued with them, calling them silly cunts. That was why he got kicked out of the painters' union.

As you know, I'm a professional writer. Once I wrote a story about my elder uncle, saying that he was a novelist and a mathematician who had all kinds of fantastic experiences. That story got me into trouble. Somebody checked my census register and discovered that I had only one uncle. This uncle attended elementary school at seven and middle school at thirteen, graduated from the oil painting department of an art school, and now was an idler with no profession. They also checked his grades from elementary school through middle school; the best grade he got in math was a "C." If he had become a mathematician, it would have definitely stained the reputation of our country's mathematical circles. For that reason, the leader had a talk with me, assigning me a plot along the following lines: when my uncles were born, they were twins. Because my grandparents were poor and couldn't afford to raise them, the older one was sent to another family. This older one had a talent for math and could make up stories and write, too, very different from my young uncle. So he and my young uncle had to be twins from different eggs. The plot also offered an explanation for this: my deceased grandmother was a native of Laixi in Shandong Province, where the water has a special ingredient that makes women produce lots of eggs. So, just because my grandmother was from Laixi, she was turned into a female yellow croaker fish. The leader intended to make me revise the story according to a plot of his own, but I refused to do it—my grandmother raised me and I have deep feelings for her. And I also believed that as a writer I could have as many uncles as I wanted. It was nobody else's business. Therefore, I committed an error, and my writing permit was revoked—I've written about this in another story and I don't want to get into it again.

At the time I'd go to pick up my young uncle, my mother was still living. My uncle had a divergent strabismus problem, both of his eyes looked outward at the same time; but they were a little better than a carp's. My mother's eyes had the same sort of problem. Looking at her reflection in the mirror, my mother thought herself beautiful in every way except her eyes. She blamed this on my young uncle. Since she was born before my young uncle, it was difficult to understand how he was to blame. She was a schoolteacher, and the subject she taught didn't have much to do with art. However, as my young uncle's sister, she thought she ought to understand him better. One day, she told my uncle, Let's see some of your paintings. But my uncle said, Forget it. Even if you saw them you wouldn't understand. My mother particularly hated when someone said there were things in the world she couldn't understand. So she flung her plate on the table and said, Fine, I won't look at them even if you beg me. You'd better be careful. Don't ask me to bail you out when you get into trouble again. My young uncle stayed silent for a while, then walked out of our house and never came back. It had been my mother's responsibility to pick up my uncle from the police station, and afterward, she refused to do her duty. But my uncle still got into trouble, as always. When he got into trouble, he would be put in the police station, and, like our mail in the post office, pick-up had to be on time otherwise we would have to pay a late fee. So I had no choice but to go there.

I have longed for love since childhood. My first sweetheart was my young uncle. Even today, I still feel embarrassed about this. My uncle was very attractive when he was young; he had dark, shiny, thick hair and smooth, taut skin; his body was bony but muscular; when he stood naked, he looked like a thoroughbred, with his broad shoulders and small hips; his penis was big but firm—I didn't really know about this last matter since I'm a man, and I'm not gay. So you should check with my young aunt.

I had skinny arms and legs when I was little; my knees could bend backward, so could my elbows; I had a pointy mouth and a monkey's hollow cheeks, and what's more, I still had my foreskin, although it was hidden in my underwear, out of view. One day I picked up my young uncle from the police station. It was a hot day, and we were both sweating like pigs. He stood by the road, trying to flag down a cab. He said he was going to take me swimming, which made me so happy I started to daydream. Just then, I got a kick at the back of my knees. Stand straight, my young uncle said. That meant my knees were bending and I was getting shorter. They tell me that when I bent my knees, I looked almost three inches shorter. After a while, I got another kick, which meant I was shrinking again. I didn't understand why it mattered to him that I got shorter, so I stared at him. My young uncle said ferociously, You look really obnoxious that way! I did love my uncle, but the bastard was not nice to me. That really hurt my feelings.

My uncle had divergent strabismus. I suppose in his eyes the world must look like a wide-screen movie, which should have helped his career; from the scientific perspective, if the eyes are far apart, their depth perception should be more acute, and they would gauge distance more precisely. In the early twentieth century, before laser and range radar were invented, people had already used this principle in measuring distance; they installed two camera lenses on the ends of a pole, about ten yards in length. Since a human being's eyeballs can't be that far apart, the improvement to vision by inducing divergent strabismus would be limited.

After a while, a cab came to take my young uncle and me to Yuyuan Lake. The lake water gave off a fishy smell that came from the mud. My young uncle said that every winter several human skeletons would be found in the mud after the water was drained. It made me feel that below my body, on the lake bottom, corpses were swelling like sponges and then dissolving into the dark green water. For that reason, I was afraid to put my head under water. Having scared me sufficiently, my young uncle swam off and began eyeing the figures of the girls on the shore. From what I saw, the girls' bodies were average; the ones with really first-rate bodies didn't come to the lake. No matter how unhappy I was, I finally got the chance to see my young uncle's body. He did have a big tool. After he got out of the water, the top of his penis was waterlogged and pale as a mushroom. Later, that pale penis was imprinted on my mind. In my dream that night, my young uncle kissed me. I scrubbed my lips after I woke up—it was a nightmare of course. I believed that pale penis was a kind of threat to the world. When my young uncle got out of the water, his lips had turned dark purple and his eyes were bloodshot. He threw me a ten-yuan bill, telling me to take a taxi back on my own, and then staggered away himself. I pocketed the money and carefully followed him, walking toward the Great Earth coffee shop, toward danger. Because I loved my uncle, I couldn't let him take the risk alone.

My uncle often went to the Great Earth coffee shop, and so did I. Built in the mid-twentieth century, it was a tile house with a steep tile roof and barred wooden windows on three sides. People said it used to be a grocery store. After it was turned into a coffee shop, red curtains with black linings were hung on all the windows. That was why the room was so dark; if you fell asleep inside, you woke not knowing whether it was day or night outside. Only when you sat in a booth by the wall and lifted the curtain, you could see the light outside, as well as the dust covering the windowsill. On every table a cheap white candle burned, with dark smoke curling up and spreading the bitter smell of paraffin wax. If you stayed too long, your nostrils would have a layer of black stuff. But, if you came to a table lit with a yellow candle that had no smoke and no smell, that was my uncle's—like me he couldn't stand the smoke of the paraffin wax, so he always brought his own candles. People said he made these candles himself, blending them with beeswax. He always ordered a cup of coffee, but never drank it. One of the waitresses knew him very well and even had a crush on him. Every time he came, she would give him the real brewed Brazilian coffee, but only charge him for the instant kind. Still my uncle didn't drink it. She was very sad and cried in the dark.

Hoping to see for myself how my young uncle sold his paintings, I put a lot of effort into tailing him. I crawled on the dark floor of the Great Earth, wearing holes in all my sleeves and pants. When the waitresses came over, with coffee in one hand and a flashlight in the other, I had to crawl out of their way, too. Every now and then, I wasn't fast enough and tripped them. They would drop the trays and scream, Ghost! Then my young uncle would come over to grab me, pointing to the way home and spitting out a single word, "Scram!" I pretended to leave, but would sneak back a moment later and continue dragging myself along the dark floor. In the dark, I could tell there were roaches, rats, and some other animals in the coffee shop; one of them was very fluffy, like a weasel. It bit me and left a bite mark, smaller than a cat's but bigger than a rat's. The bastard's teeth were sharper than an awl. I couldn't help shouting, "Fuck!" So I got caught again. He dragged me all the way out, and then I came back. We would go around like this several times an afternoon, till even I got tired of it.

Finally, the person my uncle had been waiting for came. Stocky and bald, he constantly bowed to my uncle as if apologizing for being late. I thought he was Japanese, or a Chinese person who had lived in Japan for years. They began talking in whispers, and my uncle even showed him some color photographs. I believed he was hammering out a deal, but I saw neither paintings nor money—the two things I really wanted to see. Otherwise, I couldn't claim that I had seen through the artist's tricks. After they walked out of the coffee shop, I went on tailing them. Unfortunately, my uncle always caught me at that point; he would hide by the door or behind the little street vendor's stand, grab my collar in one motion and beat me half to death—the guy was very alert. They were about to close the deal, which could be a risky moment for both the people and the booty. That was why they kept checking around. While trailing my young uncle, one had to consider his carplike eyes. With a wider field of vision than ordinary people, he could see behind him without turning around. But one thing I never figured out: how did the police get him? They must have been more observant than I was.

One day, I ran into that Japanese guy on the street. He wore a striped suit and held a tall woman's arm; the woman wore a green silk cheongsam and had a straight figure and a vigorous way of walking. But her skin seemed rough, and a little old-looking, too. I glanced at her face, noticing that the space between her two eyes was very wide. Struck by this, I decided to follow her. She squatted down to fix her high heels, and grabbed me as I passed. Out of her mouth came my young uncle's voice, Shit head, how come you're following me again? Besides the voice, she also gave off my young uncle's unique body odor. I'd suspected she was my young uncle from the beginning, and now was completely sure. I said, Why are you doing this? He said, Cut the nonsense! I'm just selling my paintings. If you keep following me, I'll strangle you! As he said this, he squeezed my shoulder hard, his fingers clamping my flesh like two steel hooks. Anyone else would have shouted at the top of his voice, but I could take it. I said, OK, I won't follow you anymore, but you better not get caught dressed like this. After he loosened his grip, I suggested that he put on a pair of sunglasses—his appearance really worried me. Honestly, if he'd brought me along, I could at least have kept an eye out for him. But my young uncle preferred taking his chances on his own rather than get me involved. If he'd gotten arrested that time, it would not only be illegal trading, but also a case of perversion. I also heard that once my young uncle hung four pieces of cardboard on his body and squatted on the street pretending to be a mailbox; the Japanese guy, dressed as a postman, went to do the deal with him. But I wasn't an eyewitness—a policeman told me. Another time, he pretended to be a high school student, volunteered to sweep the floor at a McDonald's, and hid his paintings in a garbage can; the Japanese disguised himself as a garbage collector to pick up the paintings. These were the times they got caught, which was how I heard. But my young uncle didn't get caught every time, otherwise, he'd have had no income and would've had to live on air.

Once I took a trip to Mount Hundred Flowers and saw some locals standing by the road inviting sightseers to tour the mountain on their little donkeys. A weird idea flashed through my mind: if my young uncle disguised himself as a donkey and the Japanese were a tourist riding on his back, they could bargain as they toured the mountain. So whenever I saw a donkey, I slapped its butt—I believed if the donkey were my uncle, he would definitely not allow me to spank him. He would stand up like a human being and fight me—the donkeys didn't respond much, so it seemed none of them was my uncle. But the owners were hot to fight me, and said, Hey kid! Where did you get to be so free with your hand? It looked like my uncle hadn't come up with the idea, which was good. I wouldn't like anybody to ride my uncle. I didn't tell them that I was looking for my uncle; they wouldn't have believed me anyway. That was how I toured Mount Hundred Flowers.

For a while I really wanted to open up to my uncle: You don't have to dodge me. I love you. But I never spoke up—I was afraid of his fists. Besides, I also felt these words would be too shocking and unconventional. My young uncle's eyes were wide set, and his gaze was sleepy looking, which fooled people about his reach. Of course, only someone regularly tricked by him would understand this. I often thought I was out of danger, but still he would trip me with one kick. I heard that twentieth-century kung fu master Bruce Lee was also good at this, but I am not sure whether he had divergent strabismus or not.

Uncle Policeman said that one good thing about my uncle was that he never tried to run away when he got dragnetted. Instead, he walked toward the flashlight and said: Well, you got me again! They said: Your young uncle deserves to be called an artist. He's an honorable man, not petty at all. "Dragnet" is a police word, signifying a raid done by a large number of officers. As I understand it, the word came from catching fish with a net in the river. Under this circumstance, fish usually flop around—these are the petty ones. If the fish lie at the bottom of the net without moving at all, then we would call them honorable fish. Unfortunately, most aquatic vertebrates of this kind are petty. That's why they are considered low class. An honorable fish like my uncle would always have some cash on him, which usually came from selling his paintings and would eventually be confiscated by the policemen. If the matter had ended there, it would have been convenient for both sides. But doing things like that would have meant committing errors. The correct procedure was to confiscate my uncle's illegal take first, and then bring him to the police station for correction. Since my young uncle was an honorable man, he would go with them without arguing. I always believed if my young uncle had run off then, Uncle Policeman probably wouldn't have chased him—because he had no money on him. My young uncle thought what I said made sense, but still didn't want to run away. He thought of himself as a man with social status, not a little burglar. Running away like that would be beneath him. An honorable man would be taken to the police station and often badly treated. And a genuine low-down little burglar would feel quite comfortable there, like a fish in water.

Uncle Policeman said even riding a bicycle requires a permit, never mind painting. After hearing this, my uncle said nothing, just puffed up his cheeks and swallowed air. Soon his belly swelled like a balloon. Puffing himself up was his special talent, which had very profound implications. We all know that in the past, when people killed a hog, they always inflated it first, and then used a primitive technique to remove its hair. There is also a saying that a dead hog is not afraid to be scalded by boiling water, which indicates stoicism. My uncle puffed himself up in order to show that he was a dead hog, unafraid of boiling water. Afterward, he squatted by the wall with his belly inflated, waiting for a family member to pick him up. This should have been my mother's job, but she refused to come. So I had no choice. I was a little boy when I crossed the dusty streets of the last century, walking toward the police station to pick up my uncle; I also thought to myself, Hurry up! Or young uncle will explode—it wouldn't look nice if his intestines burst through his belly. Actually, I was worried for no reason: at a certain point of inflation, the pressure inside would be too great, and my young uncle would automatically have deflated. Then, with a *puh* sound, all the sheets of paper in the police station would have blown into the air, and with the force of the strong flow, my young uncle's larynx would have emitted the sound of being scraped with a knife. After that, he would have flattened of course, spreading out on the ground like a fried pancake, making it impossible for the policemen to kick him. They could only stamp on him, and they would have said as they stamped on him: You artists are really low. I'm not just fond of artists; I also like policemen. I always think if either disappeared art wouldn't exist.

When I was little, we lived near Yuan Ming Garden, where a black market hid in a stand of poplar trees next to the boundary wall. Nearby lay a half-drained pond, with a patch of withered reeds beside it. On summer evenings, the darkness always settled in the woods first because of the lush, dense foliage; in fall, leaves dropped from the trees like heavy rain. To get into the garden required a ticket, but you could save money by jumping over the wall. Packed down by thousands of footsteps, the ground in the woods shone like the surface of porcelain; white cloths with words written in red on them were strung between the trees as signs. The market had the feel of a country village, with peasant types selling phony antiques there. But if you had a good eye, you could buy the real stuff, just dug out of graves—though I began to feel uneasy about the selling of dead people's stuff. Among these fakers, a few people wore corduroy jackets and sat on folding stools, staring blankly at their own paintings that no one bothered to ask about from morning to evening. That was why they had a melancholy look. People passed by and threw them coins. They didn't move, or thank the passersby. But a few minutes later, the coins disappeared. For a while, I went there frequently to see those people; I liked that sort of mood, believing that the people sitting there with blank looks were all great painters like Van Gogh—this type of loneliness and melancholy I envied to the point of craziness. I wished my uncle could sit with them, because he had that melancholy disposition. He would have looked good sitting there, not to mention that he could have faced a pool of gloomy, stagnant water. When spring came, the lake's surface would grow algae, like a dense, green garbage dump. The water would turn sticky and thick because of this, and waves wouldn't come up no matter how hard the wind blew. I thought he was especially right for the place, not only would he look good there, but he could also collect some spare change. I neglected to consider whether or not he would like this himself, though.

After I got my uncle, we walked on the street. He let me walk in front of him, which was not a good sign. Then I mentioned the black market for art near my house, and how people sold all kinds of fake antiques, calligraphy, and paintings. Also, there were some street artists who set up their booths on the ground. Moreover, Yuan Ming Garden police station was very close to my house, and it would be much easier for me to pick him up. But I didn't say the words "pick up," afraid that he might not be happy to hear them. He didn't say anything after listening to me, and we walked for another while. All of a sudden, he stuck out a leg and tripped me, letting me fall on the concrete, scraping my knees and elbows. And then he pulled me up and said with phony concern, My good nephew, be careful while you're walking. From this I gathered that the black market in Yuan Ming Garden was very low class. My uncle thought it would disgrace him socially if he sold his paintings there. Always quiet, my uncle was as treacherous as a cobra. But I liked him, maybe because we were alike.

There were many benefits in sending a child to pick up lawbreakers, the most important of which was to reduce the policemen's long-windedness. When a policeman faced such a young audience, his desire to talk would naturally drop off a lot. In the beginning, I rode a mountain bike to get there, calling the policemen "Big Uncle" and filling them with sweet talk until my uncle came out; later, I wore a corduroy jacket, sat quietly in the reception room waiting for him to come out. I had reached the age where policemen who liked talking finally got their chance, but my silence made them unsure of what to say. When we really had nothing to say, we would talk about how the price of rice was going to rise again, and how the crickets from Wan An public cemetery were pretty good at fighting because they fed on dead people's flesh. I said, of course, crickets couldn't be tougher than rats no matter how good they were at fighting. The policeman said it's illegal to fight rats because they spread plague. Well, since it was illegal to fight rats, I shut my mouth. At first, when my uncle came out, he would pat my head and give me a little bit of money as a tip; later, neither of us said anything, we just walked off in different directions—by that time, I didn't need his money and was afraid of his tripping me, too. That period lasted for five or six years. I grew nine inches and he was unable to pat my head anymore, unless he stood on tiptoe. I used to think that when I was seventy or eighty, I would still have to go to the police station with the help of a cane to pick up my uncle. But things took a turn for the better—they sent him to the Art Reeducation Institute. The course of study was three years, which meant I wouldn't have to pick up him for at least three years. The Art Reeducation Institute was especially set up for Bohemian artists. They could learn to be engineers or agricultural technicians at the place. Doing so would subtract one troublemaker and add one useful person, society benefiting both ways. I hear that on pig farms, if there are too many stud pigs, they castrate some and turn them into porkers—this isn't an appropriate analogy of course. I also hear that the genders are out of balance among the Chinese right now; there are more men than women. Some have proposed that the government turn a segment of the male population into females by performing sex-change operations—this also is an inappropriate analogy. Indeed, an excess of artists is a trouble to society. The numbers should be reduced. But it would be a mistake to subtract my uncle. If there are too many stud pigs, we should castrate some, but we also need to save some for stud; if there are too many men, we can castrate some, but we must save some. If we castrate all of them, we'd have to propagate the race by asexual reproduction, and the entire society would degenerate back into the fungus era. In art, my uncle was definitely a stud. It wouldn't be right to castrate him.

2

Before getting into the Art Reeducation Institute, my uncle had many lovers. I know all the details because I often sneaked into his apartment, hiding myself in the closet to steal a look. I had his key, but don't ask how I got it. My young uncle hung his paintings all over his living room. You couldn't look at them too long otherwise you got dizzy. This was another error he committed. The leader lectured him: A good piece of work should make people feel happy, not dizzy. My young uncle talked back, saying, Then, is a suppository a good piece of work? This was arguing for the sake of argument, of course. The leader was talking mood, not anus. But my young uncle was very good at arguing, and could even give the brightest leader a headache.

Each time I went to my young uncle's apartment, I would see a girl I hadn't seen before. The girl would step into his living room, look around, let out a shriek, and collapse. My young uncle had prepared special eyeglasses for his guests: he glued a piece of black paper to the lenses, leaving two small holes in the middle. After putting them on, the guest could keep her balance. She would ask, What have you painted? My young uncle's answer would be, See for yourself. The girl would study them closely, and after a while, her head would whirl again. For this situation, my young uncle prepared another set of special glasses: he glued a piece of black paper to the lenses with even smaller holes cut in the middle. After looking through these glasses for a while, the shaky feeling would return again. Finally, you put on the last set of glasses, which had no holes at all, only black paper. You saw nothing, but still felt dizzy; even with your eyes shut, those dizzying patterns would continue to float in your vision. Overcome with dizziness, those girls all fell in love with my young uncle and began to make love to him. I kept peeping through the narrow crack until the girl wore only bra and panties. And then, I would automatically close my eyes, as required by middle school regulations. Through the sounds of tender moaning, I could hear the girl still pressing, What did you paint anyway? My uncle's answer remained the same, Figure it out for yourself. I guessed that some of them might be virgins, because what they said in the end was this: I've already given myself to you. Hurry and tell me what you painted. My young uncle then said: To tell you the truth—I don't know myself. So the girl would slap his face and then my uncle would say: You can slap me, but I still don't know. So my uncle got another slap, which proved he really didn't know what he had painted. When the slapping began, I thought I could open my eyes to look again. The girls all resembled one another: they had slim figures with slender legs and arms. They all wore matched sets of knitted underwear, the upper part a bra, and the lower part, panties. The only difference lay in the decorative patterns; some had red dots against a white background, some had green horizontal stripes against a black background, and still others had white stripes against a green background. No matter what they wore, I didn't like any of them. You're not an artist or a cop? Forget about being an aunt of mine!

When my uncle went to the Art Reeducation Institute, I graduated from high school. I wanted to be an artist and didn't want to take the university entrance exam. But my mother said if I turned into a dubious character like my young uncle, she would kill me. To show her determination, she asked someone to buy six butcher knives in the Hebei countryside, sharpening them until they were snowy-bright and imbedding them in a counter in the kitchen. Every morning she made me go to the kitchen to look at them. If the knives grew rusty, she would hone them snowy-bright again. Once in a while, she would buy a live chicken and kill it, just to test the knives. After the killing, she would cook the carcass of the chicken and let me eat it. She stayed vigilant until I finished the entrance exam. A hero among women, my mother was always as good as her word. Having been scared out of my wits, I finished the exam in a complete daze and finally got into the Physics Department of Beijing University. The moral of the story is: if you fear being killed, you can't be an artist. You can only be a physicist. As you know, I'm a novelist now, which is also considered a type of artist. But it's not that I'm no longer afraid of being killed—my mother has passed away and no one is threatening to kill me anymore.

Ten years ago, I brought my uncle to the Art Reeducation Institute, carrying his bundle for him. My uncle held a big string bag himself—the sort of thing also called a basin bag. In addition to a basin, it contained a towel, a cup, toothbrush, toothpaste, and several rolls of toilet paper. We walked toward the huge iron gate. It was a cloudy day. I don't remember what we discussed on the road. Maybe I expressed envy at his being accepted there. Behind the huge gate was a big courtyard encircled by a concrete wall. The iron gate was shut tight, but a small side door was left open. Everyone had to bow in order to get in. A big crowd of students stood in front of the door, waiting to be called in, one by one. By the way, I hadn't volunteered to bring my uncle there, otherwise he would have beaten me to a pulp. The leaders required every student to be accompanied by a relative, or else he wouldn't be admitted. When our turn came, my uncle did something that clearly reveals his character back then. My uncle and I had a bit more than ten years' difference in our ages, which wasn't that much; besides that, we both wore corduroy jackets—ten years ago, people who considered themselves artists wore this type of material—I also had long hair and resembled him, too. To make a long story short, when we reached the small door, my uncle suddenly pushed me on the back, shoving me inside. By the time I realized and tried to turn my head, people inside had already grabbed my collar, yanking me as hard as if I were a stubborn bull. When they yanked me, I instinctively strained backward to get free. As a result we reached a standoff in the doorway. My jacket seams both under the arms and down the back were ripping; meanwhile, I talked myself hoarse explaining, but nobody listened. I should point out that they grabbed me thinking they had my uncle, which shows I wasn't the only one crazy about him.

The Art Reeducation Institute was located somewhere in the western suburbs of Beijing. You may gather from what I just said that the address was classified information. Right next to it was a barbed-wire fence surrounding several fish ponds. At the end of winter and beginning of spring, the fish ponds would have no water, leaving only dried, cracked mud and the lingering smell of damp sludge everywhere. A man in a blue uniform stood beside the pond. Seeing the mob, he just gawked open mouthed, unafraid of his tonsils catching a cold—that was what the place was like. I was trapped in the doorway, with my jacket hiked all the way up and the length of my back exposed. Goose bumps covered me from my ribs to my waist. But I couldn't have cared less how I looked.

Although my young uncle and I resembled one another, there were differences in our builds. Now trapped in a small iron door, with only the upper part of my body in view, these differences became less obvious. At the iron door, I protested, I'm not my young uncle. They eased their grip a little, telling someone to fetch my young uncle's picture so they could compare. After comparing they said, Aha, how dare you say you're not you! And then they yanked even harder. As the result of the yank, my jacket immediately disintegrated. Meanwhile, I began to wonder: What did they mean by "How dare you say you're not you!" The strange part about this sentence was that you couldn't actually refute it. I might have said, "I'm myself, but I'm another person." Or I could have said, "I'm not myself. I'm another person." Or even, "I'm not another person. I'm myself." Or, "I'm not another person, or myself!" No matter what I said, it would have been hard to convince them, and even demonstrated that I deserved a beating.

People grabbing me by the collar in the institute's doorway turned out to be an unusual experience for me. Not only did my heart race and my breath get short, but my face and ears turned all red; and what's more, I got a full erection. The experience was absolutely the equivalent of sex. Still, I didn't want to go in. The main reason was that I didn't consider myself qualified; I was too young, lacked accomplishment, and modesty was my chief virtue. I told the people inside all of this, but they just didn't believe me. Besides, it also occurred to me that if a place was so eager to get you, you'd better not go there. You'd hardly believe it but inside the door, girls in uniform were lined up along the pathway chirping like little birds, Jolt it with a stun stick—Oh, no, that would make him stupid—Just one jolt. One jolt on it wouldn't make him stupid, and so forth. You may have guessed that the object they were arguing about was my head. With talk like this buzzing in my ears, my head began to pound. The fat girl who held my collar said, Wang Er, why don't you wise up? It's good to be inside. While she spoke, her warm breath, which had a sour smell, blew in my face. I could tell she had just eaten a fruit candy. But I was having a hard time breathing and didn't answer her. One more thing about this fat girl: because I was so close to her, I even noticed the dandruff in her hair. If I hadn't seen that, I probably would have given up and let her drag me in.

Later, the fat girl showed up in my dreams many times, her head big as a bushel, her dandruff flying around as if she had just shaken out the buckwheat stuffing of a pillow. In the dream I make love to her, but as I recall, I was pretty reluctant. Back then I was young and strong and often had nocturnal emissions. No woman had ever grabbed me by the collar before, although now it has become routine. When my wife wants to make love, she comes right up to me and grabs my collar. At home I wear a cowboy jacket, with a cowhide-reinforced collar, which is quite strong.

My young uncle's name is Wang Er, which, of course, was not given to him by my grandfather. Many people tried to persuade him to change his name, but he liked the simple brushstrokes and refused. As for me, I wouldn't use such an inelegant name just for the sake of those simple strokes. With my collar in the grasp of those people and being called by that name, I considered myself doubly unfortunate. Finally, it was my uncle who shouted, Let him go. I'm the one you want. Then they set me free. But, during the brief struggle my jacket had been completely torn apart, strips of cloth hanging off my back like flags. My bastard uncle, with a cold grin on his face, took his luggage from my back, straightened my clothes, patted my shoulder, and said, I'm very sorry, nephew. After that, he took a look around, his gaze settling for a moment on the concrete pillars on either side of the gate. They were square pillars with two big concrete spheres on top. He spat through the gap in his teeth and said, So fucking ugly. Then he ducked and went in. The people inside didn't grab him, and even made way for him—maybe their hands were tired after the battle with me. I walked home alone, with scraps of rags dangling from my back and sore muscles in my limbs and neck. But I felt relieved. After I got home, I told my mother, I've got rid of that god of plague. My mother said, Good, you did me a great favor! Needless to say the god of plague was my uncle, whose entire being carried the plague before he got into the Art Reeducation Institute.

After bringing my uncle to the Art Reeducation Institute, a strange idea occurred to me: at any rate, from now on he belongs to the institute and doesn't need me to worry about him anymore. Meanwhile, I would think about the fat girl who grabbed me by the collar, and jealousy would begin to gnaw at my heart. Later I heard that she used to arm wrestle stevedores, had married twice and, now single again, wrote love letters to Japanese sumo wrestlers on a regular basis. Sumo wrestlers are strong and rich—she couldn't have been the least interested in my young uncle at the time. I was way off there. There was another instructor at the Art Reeducation Institute who was about four-and-a-half-feet tall and as thin as a lath, with pale skin, a sharp nose, a pointy chin, sleep crust at the corners of her eyes, and sparse hair combed into two braids. She wasn't interested in my young uncle either. Fifty-two years old already, this instructor was an old maid and had made up her mind long ago that she would devote her life to special education in our country. Between these two extremes, there were all sorts of other female instructors, but none of them was interested in my uncle. My uncle was a person of few words, peculiar in many ways. Very few people liked him. His criminal dossier contained photographs of his paintings. To be fair, those photos looked nicer than the originals since they were small, but when it came to making people dizzy they worked equally well. From these pictures alone people concluded my uncle was an obnoxious man. It seemed no one liked my uncle. I had no reason to worry.

There were all kinds of avant-garde artists at the Art Reeducation Institute; among them were poets, novelists, filmmakers and, of course, painters. In the moral education class every morning, the students' poetry and prose would be read aloud—if there were no poetry and prose to be read aloud, the instructors would show slides, and then ask the artists to explain what their work meant. Of course, these people were stubborn and wouldn't admit their mistakes: It's art—outsiders wouldn't get it! But the institute knew how to cure stubbornness—for example, by beating their heads with a club. Once the artist stopped being stubborn, he began to sweat profusely and go on the defensive, and humbled a bit then, he would admit he just wanted to impress people with claptrap, so he could become famous. Then the instructor ran a student's movie, which was not just a mess but disgusting. Without being asked, the student already felt embarrassed and automatically bowed his head for a beating. He said that he had made the movie for foreigners, intending to lighten their pockets. Unfortunately, this tactic didn't work at all with my young uncle. After the instructor showed the slides of his work, he would frankly admit before anyone asked, I don't know what I painted either. That's exactly why I painted them. So other people can appreciate them. After that, all the instructors got headaches trying to figure out how to put him on the defensive.

Everybody knew that there must be some meaning in his paintings and tried to force him to say so. He himself also agreed that his paintings must mean something, but he said, I don't know what it is. I'm too dumb. According to the leaders at the institute, all students were fools who thought they were smart. Since my young uncle refused to think he was smart, the leaders believed on the contrary that he was not a fool, but a smart-ass.

I often went to the Art Reeducation Institute to visit my young uncle. The leaders asked me to persuade him not to play dumb. They also said, Playing dumb with us won't help him. I defended my uncle saying, My young uncle isn't playing dumb—he was born dumb. But the leaders said, Don't play games with us. Playing games won't help your young uncle.

Aside from my uncle, the only other relative I had was a distant cousin. He was older than my uncle; when I was ten, he was already over forty. He had a groove in his upper lip wider than a playing card, a big hole in the seat of his pants that revealed his pubic hair as well as his balls, and a face very much resembling a bird's. Back then he lived in Sand River town, often scuffing along in midsummer in a pair of padded shoes, which were already in shreds and tatters, brandishing a slingshot made from a rubber tourniquet, and, with a broad smile, inviting the passing children to hit the hornet's nest with him—a hornet's nest is a kind of hive built on a tree that looks like a lotus seedpod. My cousin had an earnest, bass voice. He was very popular among the townspeople, always busy going in and out of the police station and the neighborhood committee. If you asked him to push the wheelbarrow or take out your garbage, he would never refuse you. Once, I brought him along to visit my young uncle, just to let the leader see there was another sort of person in our family. Who would have expected the leader to laugh after seeing my cousin? He pointed at my nose and said, You little rascal! You're really slippery! My cousin blurted out in his droning voice, Who's slippery? I'll kick his butt for him! Whenever my cousin came to the institute, he always seemed to be in high spirits; first he took all the garbage out, and then knocked down all the hives, making the hornets fly around so nobody could venture outside. He himself was stung and swelled up as big as a barrel. Despite the fact that he knocked down hives, the people at the institute all liked him very much. Not long after he went home, a passing coal truck hit and killed him. Everybody felt sad and, from then on, began to hate Shanxi people, because Shanxi Province was famous for its coal. While preparing for his funeral, the townspeople invited my mother to attend as a family member of the deceased. She felt slightly uncomfortable, but didn't refuse. Had it been my uncle, my mother might not have gone. I also told my uncle about my cousin's death. He drew a blank—couldn't remember who he was; and then it suddenly dawned on him, Look at my memory! He's been here knocking down hornet's nests. My young uncle also said he really wanted to go to my cousin's memorial service, but it was too late. My cousin had already been cremated.

After the moral education class, my uncle went to his special course. From what I saw through the window, their classroom didn't look much different from the auditoriums in our school—the same bluish fluorescent lightbulbs hanging down from the ceiling, and the same long tables and benches arranged in rows, except there were more slogans on the walls. Another difference was that their windows were fitted with iron bars and mesh, along with a sign with lightning bolts on it, warning of electricity. The sign didn't lie—I'd often see a lizard crawling over the window, then, all of a sudden, with a puff of black smoke, the lizard turned into a piece of charcoal; another time I saw a butterfly land on the window and then after a hiss, all that remained was a pair of wings floating through the air. My uncle responded to every question before anyone else just to show the instructors that he knew none of the answers. So the institute made him wear a straitjacket. After that he could take notes, but couldn't raise his hand and disturb the class. Though he couldn't raise his hand, he still talked too much. Then they put a bandage over his mouth, which he could remove only after class. Pulling it on and off plucked his beard out and made him look like a eunuch. I observed his strange appearance from the window: his left hand was tied beneath the right armpit, his right hand beneath the left armpit, and his whole torso looked just like a canvas bag; but he stared very hard, which made his eyes almost pop out of their sockets. Whenever he heard the instructor asking questions, he would get excited and snort through his nostrils. If he snorted too much, the instructor would come over and give him a shock on the head with a baton. After the shock, he would lie down and doze off. Sometimes, remembering his old habit from the police station, he tried to puff himself up. But the canvas strait-jacket was so hard to burst that it forced his body into a spindle shape—by that time his face would turn the color of liver. The air made him very uncomfortable, and he had to release it—there was a hole in the bandage especially for that purpose—then the person sitting in front of him would turn around and hit him on the head, You smell like a horse, you son of a bitch!

The institute leaders lavished care on their students; they prepared a pair of thick glasses for each student, allowing them to wear the glasses even before they became nearsighted, made them brown wool and polyester suits as the institute's uniform, and equipped everyone with a big leather briefcase, which they were not permitted to hold by the handles but had to carry on their chests. They said the students would appear more sincere by carrying their briefcases that way. The course load was very heavy, eight classes during the day and homework in the evening. To prevent the students from misbehaving, stocks were installed on every desk, in order to force them to bend over the desk. So after a while, all of them looked like bookworms—that is, they all had stooped backs and bent necks, wore brown suits and held big briefcases in front of them; their glasses resembled the bottom of bottles, their heads were so smooth and shiny that even flies would slide down the surface—unfortunately they were studious in name but not in action, what's more, they drooled out of the corner of their mouths. My uncle drooled the most, his saliva gurgling down almost like a stream. Even if the food at the institute hadn't been tasty enough and he were ravenous for steamed buns and meat, he couldn't have drooled any worse. People generally believed that he did this on purpose, trying to blacken the reputation of the institute's food. To stop his drooling, they stopped offering him water to drink, and even made him eat dry red pepper. But none of these methods worked. The only difference those methods made was that the color of his saliva changed; now it was burnt yellow, like the urine of someone suffering from too much yang.

It was a very natural idea to let painters who had no permits, such as my uncle, study to be engineers. You might think they'd have some talent for drafting; unfortunately, though plenty were sent there, few succeeded. Almost every painter without a permit regarded himself a genius like Picasso. Imagining he could do anything else besides painting, such as dispensing toilet paper, would be an insult to him, never mind becoming an engineer. Because of this, none of them did any drafting while they were locked into the stocks on their desks. Some of them drew little cats and dogs, and others drew little chickens and ducks. One guy didn't even know what he was drawing—that guy was my uncle. Later these drawings were used as the engravings on paper money because they were impossible to counterfeit. The paper money in our country used to be designed by painters with permits, whose drawings could be faked by any peasant who had a little training in Chinese folk painting. But the works of the students at the institute all looked very strange, blurred with lots of faint stains that no one could forge unless his head and hands were also locked into stocks on a drafting table. The faint stains were drool marks, associated with the shape of their lips and the state of their salivary glands. These were almost impossible to imitate. My uncle's drawings had more stains than lines, like a baby's diaper. So they were passed off as the ink-wash lotus paintings of Qi Baishi, and engraved on five hundred-yuan bills. By the way, as my uncle drew these, his head and hands were stretched in front of him, and his waist and legs behind, like an old wolf caught in the freeze-frame of a cartoon. When the drafting teacher passed behind him, he gave my uncle a shock to the head and said, Convict Wang (that was how they addressed the students there), stop being a water pipe! The teacher thought he drooled too much. Because of the drooling, my uncle was thirsty all the time and had to drink constantly. After a while he became like Pavlov's dogs, starting to drool as soon as he heard the bell ring for class.

I heard that the most difficult students at the institute were the ones in mechanical drawing (namely, those who painted without a permit). As we all know, everybody can write; when you arrange the words in lines, it's poetry; in paragraphs, it's fiction; in dialogue, it's drama. Therefore, it was pretty easy for poets, novelists, and playwrights to admit that they were nothing special. However, things were quite different with painters. For instance, if you gave a layman some colors, he didn't even know where to start. Besides, every painter had his own idol, such as the French Impressionists at the end of the century before last and the beginning of the last century. If you called an artist a loafer, he would reply, People said the same thing about Van

Gogh. Our country still had diplomatic relations with France, so it was improper to denounce Van Gogh severely. But the institute had its own way of dealing with these people: the instructor collected the students' works from the drafting class, made them into slides, and then displayed them in the moral education class. Meanwhile, the instructor would ask: Convict so and so, what did you paint? The student answered: Reporting to the Instructor, it's a cat! Then the instructor would show a picture of a real cat, and the next sentence would make the convict want to sink through the floor, Now, let's all take a look. See what a real cat looks like! After this sort of reeducation, that student would shed his pride and settle down to drafting. But such tactics didn't work on my uncle. When his ink-wash lotus painting was shown, he stood up and said, Reporting to the Instructor, I don't know what I painted! The instructor had to continue, What are these bright scribbles? My young uncle answered, That's my dried-up saliva. The instructor questioned him again, Does saliva look like this? My uncle replied, Permission to ask the Instructor, what do you think saliva should look like? Unable to find a picture of saliva, the instructor could do nothing but put the bandage over my uncle's mouth again.

A month after he got in, the institute tested the students' IQ. The testee was tied to a custom-made measuring apparatus, which was also an electric torture machine. What was tested could be either the testee's IQ or his ability to withstand torture. The thing consisted of two big iron boxes, one above and the other one below, supported by a steel frame. In the middle was a light stretcher that could be moved on a slide. Some leather straps were attached to the frame of the stretcher. Before the testee got onto it, the stretcher had to be pulled out first and the testee's limbs would be tied with the leather straps, forcing his body into the shape of a cross; then he would be pushed inside—the rectangular steamer in our school's kitchen, with its drawers one over another, looked a little like this machine—If the testee were not tied, you couldn't test his IQ precisely. In order to test the students' IQs precisely, the institute first called a meeting to discuss what scores the students' IQs should be in order to conform to reality. The instructors all agreed that these students were wild and stubborn. If the institute allowed their IQs to appear too high, it wouldn't advance their thought reform. But my uncle was a special case. He always played dumb. To allow his IQ score to be too low wouldn't advance his thought reform either.

Later, my uncle told me that he'd circled around the measuring apparatus several times, trying to find the plate that indicated which factory manufactured it, but failed. From the crude metalwork, he could tell it was made in China. Therefore, he reached the conclusion that the machine used to have a plate, but it was removed—there was the evidence of a mark that supported this idea—for fear the students would blow up the factory after they were released. The machine also had two electrodes, meant to be placed on the testee's body. If the electrodes were placed too low, pubic hair would burn; if too high, the hair on the head would burn. Put simply, some hair was going to burn. When the canteen bought pigs' heads and knuckles with the bristle not completely removed, they would send them over and let the machine do that job, too. As a result the IQ of a pig's head was determined to be higher than an artist's, but a knuckle's was a bit lower. To make a long story short, when the machine operated, it always smelled of burned bristle. Any other smell was caused by the ones who forgot the posted slogan: Toilet before testing. An arrow after the slogan pointed in the direction of the toilet. Like the door of a bank vault, the toilet door was equipped with a timer lock. It would shut you in for half an hour once you entered. A stereo inside played popular music—music of this sort worked to encourage people to defecate and urinate faster.

At the test, the students usually made the request of the instructors: we'll be dating women later, so please leave us our pubic hair. But sometimes the instructor operating the machine would say: I want to leave the hair on your head. This was because the instructors at the institute were innocent and sincere girls. Some of them already had feelings for their students and hoped to maintain their good looks by saving the hair on their heads and to prevent them from sewing their wild oats by burning their pubic hair. Besides that, the instructor would advise her student outside the machine: Why don't you answer fewer questions right? Don't let the shock make you stupid. To be frank, this advice might not keep his IQ down, because most probably he'd act like a skinny donkey squeezing out a hard turd—determined to play the tough guy. He would rather put up with the electricity than answer the questions wrong. By the time the test was over, the student often collapsed in a ball. There were always touching scenes where an instructor, weeping and sobbing, carried her student out on her back.

The scene of the IQ test was very exciting. From the ceiling an incandescent light hung down, the bulb was very small, but the shade was big, which made it look like a loudspeaker. The lightbulb lit the lower part of the room but not the ceiling. The instructor brought her student in, pulled out the stretcher with a bang and gave her terse order: Take off your clothes. Lie down there. Then she turned around and put on her white lab jacket and a pair of rubber gloves. The room was very cold. Taking off clothes caused goose bumps. Some would crack a joke at this moment, but my uncle was a quiet person, always keeping his mouth shut. There were leather belts inside, and the instructor began tying the student tightly, tying him like Jesus on the cross—with his arms outstretched and two legs held together, left foot under the right. A talker would say, Why so tight? I'm not a pig! The instructor would reply, It would save us a lot of trouble if you were a pig. After being tied up, most students would get a hard-on. The instructor would say, Still misbehaving at a moment like this? And the student would argue, I'm not misbehaving. He's always this big! The instructor said, Don't brag! Then she would push him in with a rumble. While lying in the drawer, my uncle would get a hard-on, too. But he wouldn't reply to the instructor's questions. The instructor would smack his belly and said, Hey, Convict Wang, I'm talking to you. Are you always this big? He would close his eyes and say, It's usually smaller. Hurry up! So he was pushed in with a rumble, too. They say the wheels under the stretcher worked really well. When someone was pushed in, he would feel himself in free fall, completely weightless; then with a huge thud, the top of his head bumped the back wall of the machine, making it ring a little. The scene gave me the creeps—I would have hated to be tied and pushed in. Of course, it would make a big difference if I were the instructor, wearing the white lab coat and tying beautiful girls to the stretcher.

They say that there was a color TV screen installed on the top of the drawer, where the questions were displayed. If the instructor liked the student, she would entertain him with an amusing videotape first, and then shock him half to death, just like a benevolent dentist gives his patient candy before pulling his teeth. However, when my uncle's turn came, there were no videotapes, no questions either, only a sharp shock that made him wail like a ghost. Everyone was a slab of ice-cold meat before being pushed in, with puffs of breath visible between his mouth and nose, and something sticking up out of his crotch like a flagpole; after being pulled out, he was steaming all over as if cooked through, although nothing smelled good in that steam, as if a piece of rotten meat had been cooked; his hair, if he had any, would curl like springs; as for the thing that stuck out, it was down of course. But it was different with my uncle; he came out still stiff, even two or three times bigger than when he went in, and people simply couldn't stand the sight of it. Some students groaned faintly when they came out, as if a horsefly or a dung beetle were buzzing around the room; some kept silent. When my uncle came out, he shouted like a crazy man, Ah, wonderful! Excellent! Very exciting! As mentioned previously, now came the time for the instructor to carry her student on her back. The way she would carry her student was very strange: she laid the student down first, held his feet on her shoulders, gave a little shout and dragged him out with his head on the ground—they say that people in slaughterhouses carry dead pigs this way. No one liked to carry my uncle. They would say, Convict Wang, don't play dead. Get up and walk! Everyone else was a dead pig, but not my uncle. My uncle actually stood up with the help of the wall, then, still wobbling, walked away.

Now it's time to talk about their scores. Most of the students scored between 110 and 100. The guy with the highest score got a 115; he bragged that it wouldn't be too difficult for him to get a 120, but he was afraid if he got the 120, he would be made very stupid because electricity could shock people into stupidity. As for my uncle, his IQ was zero—he didn't answer a single question right. This made the leaders very angry: Even a wooden stick could do better than that. So they adjusted the voltage and put him back in for a makeup test. The result of the retest was no more than 50 points. Of course, it could have been higher. But chances are my uncle would have been electrocuted. One thing you probably gathered even though I didn't mention it: other people got their shocks when they gave the right answers, and my uncle got his when he gave the wrong ones. Experienced instructors said that they weren't afraid of students who were tricky and troublemakers but dreaded dealing with someone like my uncle who played possum.

After the test, my uncle lay on his bed waxy-faced, as if he had hepatitis. I asked him how he felt then. He stared blankly for a while, then a ghostly smile appeared on his face and he said, Very good. He also told me that he had ejaculated wildly in that box. The box was such a mess that it looked like he had thrown jelly around, or a used condom. The next person couldn't help howling from inside, Fuck your mother, Wang Er! Can't you try to collect a little good karma, you son of a bitch? Maybe the guy thought the box was too unsanitary. People said that before getting into the measuring machine, anyone with a social conscience would beat off besides, emptying balls and bowels. They called this jerking off till you were drained, because you might lose control inside the box. But my uncle didn't want to do this. He said he was very excited when he got shocked. If he jerked off till he was drained, it wouldn't be that exciting. I thought he was right. He was a real artist. Real artists were guys who had no regard for anything. But I wasn't sure what was so exciting: was it the questions appearing on the screen of the measuring machine? (He managed to remember one of them: "What does eight plus seven equal?") Or the electric current that went through his body? Or the jelly he shot all over the box? But my uncle refused to answer any of my questions, only closed his eyes.

The day after the test, my young uncle didn't get up for morning exercise; nor did he respond to people calling his name. When they came back from lunch, he was still in his bed. One of his roommates reported this to the instructor. The instructor said, Just ignore him. And don't give him food either. Let's see how long he lasts! So everyone went to class. When they came back in the evening, the room was full of flies. Only then did they find that my young uncle had died and even turned a little green. The smell was really bad after they lifted the quilt. So they got a car and sent him to the hospital morgue. Then they discussed how my young uncle died, whether or not the institute should inform his family and how, et cetera. After serious discussion, they came to the conclusion that my uncle had a heart attack. He had been sent to the hospital before his death, and the doctors had tried to save him for three days and nights, at a cost of tens of thousands. But we didn't need to worry about the money since all institute students had health insurance and could get reimbursed—the advantage of living in a socialist country. Meanwhile, the institute sent a messenger to inform the hospital what they had come up with, in case we inquired about it. By the time all the lies fell into place and they were ready to inform us, the Lijiakou police station phoned, saying that they had arrested my young uncle selling his paintings without a permit at the Great Earth café again. The institute had better send someone there to collect him. This bewildered everybody at the institute. No one dared to pick him up because there were three possibilities: first, Lijiakou arrested somebody who looked like my young uncle. In that case, the institute would risk appearing stupid by sending someone on this errand, as if they didn't know my young uncle had died; secondly, the Lijiakou police station was playing a practical joke on the institute. To pick up my uncle in this situation would also appear stupid; lastly, Lijiakou police station had arrested my uncle's ghost. To send someone there would help promote national superstitiousness. I don't know which genius had the idea of going to the morgue later to check the body. Only then did they discover that my young uncle was made of pork, yellow beans, and flour. At that point the person still alive was in big trouble.

My uncle was a great painter, but this great painter had a bad habit: he liked to draw tickets. Even when he was very little, he would draw movie tickets and bathhouse tickets, anything but money; he knew counterfeiting was illegal. Occasionally he would draw a few valuable stamps. When his permit was canceled, he drew a fake permit. But now with a computer number on every ID, it would be useless for him to draw a fake permit. He could also make all kinds of phony objects. The best example was a piece of shit he made out of laundry soap when he went to a friend's house for dinner. He put the turd on the sofa, and it was so realistic that the hostess fainted at the sight of it. The guy wanted to get out of the institute, and also felt obliged to provide an explanation. So he asked me to buy fifty pounds of pork without worrying about quality. I bought half a diseased pig from the market and smuggled it into the institute in a sack. However, I had no idea that he was going to make a dead person out of it. If I'd known, I would have suggested he use soap. Putting half of a diseased pig in the dorm was too disgusting.

When I carefully examined the gains and losses of my young uncle's early life, I found that he had made many mistakes. First of all, he shouldn't have painted paintings that people didn't understand. But as he pointed out later, he wouldn't have become a painter if he hadn't painted them; secondly, he should have titled his paintings Sea Horse, Squirrel, and Snail. But he also said that he wouldn't have been a real painter if what he'd painted were sea horses, squirrels, and snails; and then he shouldn't have played dumb at the institute. According to him, not playing dumb would have given him the creeps. And life would have been intolerable. The next thing he shouldn't have done was running away and putting half of a diseased pig carcass in his bed. But my young uncle also had something to say about that: Should I have hung around waiting for another electric shock? Should I not have faked the corpse and waited till they found me? So these mistakes could be forgiven, but not the last one—he shouldn't have been painting and selling his paintings right after he escaped. If he'd just waited a few days more, only until the institute informed us that he was dead, then everything would have been all right. When Lijiakou police station informed them that they had arrested my young uncle, they might have said nothing but this: the guy is already dead; you must have arrested the wrong person. I thought my young uncle would come up with some excuses for himself, such as he couldn't wait to get back to his painting, et cetera. Who knew that he would stare blankly? He was in a daze for a long time, and then he smacked himself on the forehead, Really, I'm so stupid!

3

There are many situations in life, and I had more than one young aunt. But the one I'll be talking about here is my real young aunt. I liked my young uncle very much and hoped that he would marry many different women; I thought of one after another until Marilyn Monroe came to mind. That individual died many years ago, and her flesh and bones have turned to dust. But I hear she had a really big bust when she was alive. As I said before, my uncle had a divergent strabismus problem. So my young aunt had to have a big bust. Otherwise, with part of her bust wobbling outside his range of vision, the visual effect would be too unpleasant. As a matter of fact, I had no reason to worry. My real aunt fixed my young uncle's divergent strabismus in a single night.

A tall and slender woman, my young aunt had fair skin and a supple waist. Whether she sat in a bed or on a sofa, she liked to tilt her head so you could see her shiny dark hair. Besides that, she always seemed about to burst out laughing. The sentence she said to me most often was: Can I help you with something? This usually happened when I pretended to barge into her room by accident, and then she would have that expression on her face. Those incidents happened a lot. However, that was many years ago.

The story began as follows: we used to live on the first floor when I was little, then we moved up to the sixth floor, and the building didn't have an elevator. Inside the building were bare concrete stairs, corridors full of dust and paint peelings, garbage collecting in the corners, et cetera. To be more specific, the garbage consisted of onionskins, eggshells, and all kinds of plastic bags, which smelled terrible. Everyone wanted it clean but felt whoever did the cleaning would be a sucker. One day, heavy steps came from the stairway; then a woman's voice could be heard from outside, Convict Wang, is this the place? A man answered, Yes. As soon as I heard this, I told my mother, Damn, it's my young uncle! My mother didn't believe me, saying my young uncle had a long way to go before he got out. But I believed it, because I had a deeper understanding of my uncle's morals than my mother. We opened the door, and there he was, along with a girl in uniform, who was my young aunt. But she didn't want to let on. My uncle introduced my mother to her, This is my Big sister. My young aunt took off her hat and called, Big sister! Then he introduced me, This is my nephew. She said, Oh, really? And then she burst out laughing, Convict Wang, your nephew looks very much like you. The thing I hated most was when people said that I looked like my young uncle, but that time was an exception. I thought my young aunt was a charming woman. If I had known that getting into the Art Reeducation Institute would bring such luck with women, I would have gone instead of my uncle.

Now I want to confess that I didn't like any of my young uncle's girlfriends. But my young aunt was a special case. The first time she showed up she wore a uniform with a peaked cap, and tucked into her wide leather belt was a little pistol. She was in high spirits and looked magnificent. The way she dressed fascinated me. On the other hand, my uncle appeared in a pair of stainless steel handcuffs, holding them in front of his chest like a black bear about to take a bow. Just as there's a difference between cat and mouse, prisoner and guard should also maintain some distinctions. That is why some people wear handcuffs, and others have guns. Once they entered our apartment, my young aunt unlocked one of my uncle's handcuffs, which made me think that she had handcuffed him just to act out their roles. I didn't expect her to cuff him to a handy radiator pipe. And then she said, Big sister, I need to use your bathroom. Off she went. Unable to stand straight or squat, my uncle could only maintain a position halfway between the two, with a rather humiliated look. I was confused and didn't know what was going on. After a while, my young aunt came out, cuffed herself to my uncle and then the two of them sat on the sofa side by side. They seemed to me to be playing some sort of sexual game. In short, sometimes you need a certain sense of humor to understand life. My mother didn't have that, she understood nothing, and that was why she was often annoyed half to death. I have that sense of humor, and because of it, I found my aunt particularly charming.

As soon as I saw my young aunt, I knew she was a spirited woman who would give my uncle a hard time. But after all she was still a woman, and thankfully, not a man. On the balcony, I congratulated my uncle, telling him my young aunt was prettier than any other girls he had dated. My uncle didn't say anything, just asked for a cigarette. In my experience, when my uncle didn't want to talk, you'd better leave him alone. Otherwise he'd get you. Besides, he seemed very unhappy that day. Being cuffed to him, I wouldn't have been able to run away if he'd suddenly turned on me. He finished the cigarette, and said, I'm not sure whether it's good luck or bad. Then he added, Let's go inside. So we went back to the bedroom and asked my young aunt to take off the handcuffs. She looked us up and down, and said, Convict Wang, this little bad egg really looks like you—maybe he is as bad as you. Usually, an aunt doesn't use that sort of tone to talk about her nephew. Anyhow my uncle finished the cigarette so completely that he even smoked the butt, which showed how much he needed nicotine. Since he was a popular man, he had never been short of cigarettes any place he went. Now he was even smoking the butt, a very unusual thing. In brief, in all the time I knew him, he'd never fallen so low.

Now I must admit that my political consciousness functioned on a very low level when I was young, no better than the little girl that I met on the bus. That little girl was very clean, and only wore underpants, not even a skirt. Her not having a skirt meant her mother thought that her daughter's legs were not enough to give men ideas; her wearing underpants was because the part above the legs would give men ideas. My young aunt guarded my uncle on the bus. It was pretty late, and there were only six or seven passengers. The little girl ran up to my uncle, staring at the handcuffs he wore and asking my young aunt, Auntie, what's wrong with this uncle? My young aunt explained to her, This uncle committed an error. The child already knew whom to love and whom to hate, and, meanwhile, was aware that my uncle, being handcuffed, couldn't do anything to defend himself. So she asked for the truncheon from my young aunt, wanting to beat my uncle. My young aunt told her, Not everyone can beat an uncle who has committed an error. The girl blinked her eyes as if she didn't understand. My aunt explained again, This uncle committed the kind of error that only this Auntie can beat him for. This time, the girl got it. She screamed at my young aunt, Obnoxious! You're no fun. Then she ran away.

Speaking of political consciousness, the one with the lowest level, of course, was my uncle; next came me since I always saw things from his perspective; then it was my mother, who felt uneasy when she saw my young aunt handcuffing my uncle; next was my young aunt, forever on guard against my uncle; but the most advanced one was that little girl. Wanting to beat someone with low political consciousness was the sign of advanced political consciousness.

The error that my uncle committed might have thousands of strands, but they all came down to one thing—nobody understood his paintings. It wouldn't be too bad if that were the only problem; those paintings appeared understandable. This made people wonder whether the bait hid the hook. Now in writing this story I seem to be committing the same sort of error—the story appears understandable, but nobody can understand it. It's not my fault, but my uncle's, because that's how he was. My mother had a prejudice against my young uncle, believing he was neither like my older uncle nor like her. She thought there must have been a mistake in the delivery room. I look very much like my young uncle, so she said I was a mistake, too. But I don't think everybody can be a mistake all the time. Somebody has to be right sometimes. Anyhow, she always thought that I was the one who knew what was going on with my uncle, but that was wrong—not even my uncle knew what was going on with himself. She called me into the kitchen and said, You two are joined at the hip. Will you just tell me what's going on?

I said, Nothing. It's just my uncle has a new girl. She is a policewoman. He's getting out soon. My mother then started worrying, not about my uncle, but about my young aunt. In her eyes, my young aunt was a good girl and my young uncle wasn't a suitable match for her—my mother always paid attention to the business of mating, as if she worked in a breeding station. However, by evening she no longer worried about my young aunt, because she and my young uncle started to make love—though they were in another room and kept their door shut, we still knew what they were doing. They made noise all night, sometimes screaming, sometimes moaning. The whole building could hear them. This made my mother very angry. She slammed the front door behind her and went to stay in a hotel, taking me with her. What most angered my mother was that she thought my uncle had behaved himself in the Art Reeducation Institute and was rewarded with an early graduation (or you could call it an early release). But the truth was just the opposite: my uncle had behaved badly there and was to receive a more severe punishment. My young aunt was his escort. They were headed to a labor camp, taking the opportunity to fool around here on the way. For this reason, my mother asked me ferociously, Can you tell me what this is all about? This time even I was confused. So clearly my uncle and I were not joined at the hip.

After getting the notion about my aunt's advanced political consciousness, I was full of questions about her behavior: If you think my uncle is a bad person, why do you still make love to him? Her answer was: It's a waste not to do it—your uncle is a bad egg, but not a bad man. This is called "recycling." But she didn't say so that night. If she did, I would have told my uncle about it, and my uncle would have been on his guard—she said this much later.

The scene of my young uncle and my young aunt's lovemaking was the small sofa in my bedroom. I was certain of this because when I left the apartment the previous night, the sofa was firm and in good shape. By the time I came back, it had been turned into a mound of dough. Besides that, stuck on the wall behind the sofa were three pieces of chewed gum. I removed one of them, tasted it, and calculated that it had been chewed for at least an hour. So you can reconstruct the scene at the time: my uncle sat in the sofa, and my aunt rode him, chewing a piece of gum. Having deduced this, I thought it was such an excellent sight that I cheered and jumped over to my own bed. It was the only bed in my room, yet it had no trace of being slept in at all. I didn't suspect that my young aunt had held a gun on my young uncle. When I found out, I didn't know whether I should have been cheering or not.

Incidentally, my young aunt enjoyed making love to my uncle very much. She would get very excited and cry out every time. Then she would handcuff her left hand to my uncle, hold the pistol in her right hand, pointing it at my uncle's head—it was the real thing in the beginning, and then she switched to a toy gun after quitting her job as a guard. When she caught her breath, she would say, Tell me, Convict Wang, do you love me or do you just want to use me? To be fair, when it came to female government employees, the first thing my uncle did was to use them, and the next to talk about love. But with a gun pointed at his head, of course, he didn't dare tell the truth. Besides, it's really hard to say how much someone can enjoy lovemaking under those circumstances.

My young aunt and my young uncle were not people who spoke the same language. People who don't speak the same language could only make love that way. While making love to my aunt in our apartment, my uncle stared at the little steel thing and kept wondering: Damn it! Is the safety on or off? Where is the safety? How am I supposed to know whether it's on or not? He could have mentioned it to my aunt, but since they hadn't known each other very long, he was embarrassed to ask. By the time they were sufficiently well acquainted, he learned that the gun didn't have any bullets, which really pissed him off: he would rather have gotten killed by an accidentally discharged bullet than worry for no reason. However, the pistol fixed his eye problem. Before that, it was one eye eastward and the other westward. Staring at the gun so long corrected the problem. Only he was overcorrected and became cross-eyed.

After turning my uncle cross-eyed, my young aunt was proud of herself at first, but soon began to have regrets. She advertised for a cure in a small newspaper and received a folk prescription, which said to get a pair of cattle eyeballs—whether from a cow or a water buffalo didn't matter, but they had to be an actual pair. Then you marinated them in honey, keeping one here and sending the other to Nanjing. After calculating that the one en route was about to reach Nanjing, you ate the one in Beijing, then hurried to Nanjing to eat the other one. My aunt wanted my uncle to try it. But as soon as my uncle heard about eating cattle eyeballs, he said, I would rather die. Because he didn't use this folk prescription, his eyes remained crossed. But what if he tried the cure and the cure turned his eyes into something like a dead cow's, one eyeball pointed south and the other north?

The next morning, my mother said to my young aunt, You're sick. You should go see a doctor. She meant that my aunt came in waves when she made love. As calm as ever, my young aunt went on cracking melon seeds and said, If that's an illness, it's a good illness. Why should I try to be cured? From this answer, I judged my young aunt's mind to be clear and logical. She didn't seem sick. But after she stopped talking, she did something strange: she stood up, buckled her uniform belt, took out the handcuffs, and cuffed my uncle in a flash. She then said, Let's go, Convict Wang. It's off to the labor camp for you. No more delays. Wanting to get a few more days off, my uncle began to play for time. But my aunt raised her eyebrows and stared at him, saying, Don't waste your breath! She also said, Love is love, and work is work. She was very firm about this and not wanting to get mixed up with a criminal—that was how she took my uncle away. This incident nearly drove my mother mad. She was cut off in her prime, and my young aunt was to blame.

4

In the last century there was a big alkali factory near Bo Sea, famous for its Triangle Brand of pure alkali. To this day when you pass through the Lutai area, you can still see a mass of gray factory buildings. Because the ammonia soda process consumed too much electricity, the alkali factory had closed. Now the alkali people needed had to be dug from the alkali field. It's a hard job, but fortunately there are people who commit errors and need to be reeducated, so the work is left to them. Besides them, some innocent people are also needed to stand guard. That's the prologue to this story. My uncle has survived the labor camp, so what will happen to him is hard to say. Anyhow, my uncle dug alkali on the alkali field, and my aunt guarded him. The alkali field is not far from Lutai. Every time I passed through Lutai, I could see those empty gray factory buildings. Numerous sea birds flew in and out of the big holes left by the removal of the doors and the windows. They blocked the sky and covered the ground. The deserted factory had become a huge birdhouse, and people shaved bald as a gourd and wearing shackles walked in and out, taking shovels and carts with them. This meant that the hard labor not only consisted of digging alkali, but also scraping up bird shit. I heard that in addition to becoming fertilizer, the bird shit could also be used as a food additive. It needs processing of course—you can't eat it untreated.

Every time I went to the alkali field, I always rode on the bus with the blue roof. Between the word "factory" and the word "field" there's little difference, but they were not located in the same place. The bus clanked along the deserted railroad, with puffs of dark smoke rushing out of its long, thin iron chimney. If the bus broke down halfway, everyone had to get off to push. The passengers walked on the road to push the bus, and the driver sat in the bus to fix the engine. On several unfortunate occasions, we had to push it all the way to our destination. We would pass many empty train stations, shunts not in use anymore, and very ugly, rusty rails. The walls of the stations were full of slogans, such as "Protect All Railroad Equipment," "Crack Down on Railway Property Theft," and so forth. But the doors and windows had all been stolen. What was left were the shells of the buildings, like skulls, where bats, wild rabbits, and hedgehogs lived. A hedgehog wears gray and has two pairs of bowlegs. I envy the hedgehog's lifestyle very much: it idles the time away, hunts for food and, meanwhile, enjoys the sunshine, as long as it avoids its born enemy, the weasel. Every time I visited the alkali field, my socks would turn rusty. I really had no idea how the rust got into them.

When I went to the alkali field to visit my young uncle, I always felt a little awkward. My young aunt and uncle were a couple. Whoever I meant to visit, it wouldn't seem quite right. If I intended to visit both of them it would make me look like a low type; if I went to see neither, why go? My only comfort was that my uncle and I were both artists; for one artist to visit another should be all right. But this raised a big problem: I didn't know what art or an artist was. In this case, to claim both my uncle and I were artists wasn't too convincing.

The railroad in the alkali field led all the way to the center of a tent city. Guarded by two wooden watchtowers, the tents were encircled by barbed wire. In the middle of the tent city was a dirt yard, littered with yellow clay and stones. At noon the stones would gleam like glacial debris. The bus drove right into the yard. A wooden platform stood in the very center of the yard. At first glance you wouldn't know the purpose of the platform. As soon as my uncle arrived, they asked him to lie on the front part of the platform and stretch out his legs. Then they got a pair of big shackles and bolted them on his legs. By the time they finished the riveting, the purpose of the platform was clear. The main part of the shackles consisted of an iron chain, about forty pounds in weight and several yards long. Lying on the ground and looking at the big iron chain, my uncle considered it overkill. He also thought the chain was too cold, so he said, Reporting to the Instructor, is this necessary? I just painted a few paintings. My young aunt said, Don't worry. Let me go ask someone. A few minutes later, she came back and said, I'm terribly sorry, Convict Wang. There is no smaller chain—you said you had only painted a few paintings. There is someone here who just wrote one poem. Hearing this, my uncle had nothing to say. Afterward, they shaved my uncle's long hair, which he valued very much, and turned his head into a shiny bulb. Concerning his hair, I need to add something here: though his head was bald in the front, the back part remained luxuriant. This made my uncle look like an old fogey from the Qing dynasty, quite a unique style. By the time it was shaved completely bald, he looked like a simple, honest man. In desperation, my uncle cried out for help, Instructor! Instructor! They're shaving me. My aunt shouted back, Be quiet, Convict Wang. Should they be shaving me, instead of you? My uncle had no choice but to shut up. As smart as my uncle was, he should have realized at that point that something was really wrong. Right then he needed to stick to his statements about loving my young aunt. If I had been in his place, I would have done the same thing. I wouldn't have changed my words even if they beat me to death.

For my uncle's labor reform in the alkali field, he had to dig alkali every day. According to what he said later, the scene at the time was as follows: he wore a blue coat stuffed with recycled rags, dragged the big shackle, and carried a pick on his shoulder, walking on the snow-white alkali flat. The wind blew hard, and the sun glared white. If you didn't wear sunglasses, you would go snow-blind—alkali can reflect light as much as snow. From my description above, you know my uncle didn't have sunglasses, so he walked with his eyes closed. My young aunt followed him, dressed in a woolen uniform, with a pair of high leather boots and a gun belt around her waist—all of which added a heroic touch to her bearing. She pulled down her hat strings and tied them under her chin. After a while, she said, Stop, Convict Wang! There's nobody here. You can open the shackles now. My uncle squatted to unlock his shackles, and said, Reporting to the Instructor, I can't unscrew it. The screw has rusted. My young aunt said, Stupid idiot! My uncle said, Can you blame me? It has both salt and alkali in it—what he meant was that with salt and alkali, any ironware would rust quickly. My aunt said, Piss on it! It will be easier to unscrew when it's wet. My uncle said he couldn't piss. Actually he's finicky and didn't want to touch the urine-soaked screw. My young aunt hesitated for a few minutes and said, As a matter of fact, I have to pee—but never mind, let's move on. My uncle stood up, shouldered the pick, and went on walking. On the snow-white alkali flat, there was nothing but the sparse, withered yellow reeds. They walked and walked and then my aunt asked my uncle to stop again. She untied her weapon belt, hung it around my uncle's neck, walked toward a cluster of reeds and squatted there to take a pee. Then they moved on. By that time my uncle wasn't just carrying the pick, but also had a gun belt over his neck, a pistol in one hand, and a cattle prod in the other one, and tottered a lot—an entirely bizarre sight. Finally my uncle found a place where the alkali was thick. He took off his blue coat, spread it on the ground, put the gun belt beside it, then walked away and started swinging his pick and breaking up the alkali. My young aunt paced around him in circles, making constant creaking sounds, weighing the cattle prod in her hand. Then she stopped, taking a red silk scarf out of her left pocket, tying it around her neck; from her right pocket she took out a pair of sunglasses and put them on. Then she walked to the blue coat, took off all of her clothes, spread out her fair-skinned body and started to sunbathe. Soon her fair body turned red. Meanwhile, my uncle faced the chilly wind with his nose running, swinging the pick to break up the alkali. Every now and then, my young aunt would call out lazily, Convict Wang! He would throw the pick aside, rush over with a series of clanks and say, Reporting to the Instructor, Convict Wang here at your service. But my aunt had no real business; she just wanted him to look at her. With his nose running, my uncle had to bend over, squint in the cold wind and admire her for a long while. Then my aunt asked him how she looked. My uncle wiped his running nose with his sleeve and mumbled in a low and deep voice, Pretty! Pretty! My young aunt was very content and said, OK, haven't you looked at me enough? Now go back to work. My uncle then ran back with a series of clanks, thinking to himself: What does she mean by "Haven't you looked at me enough?" I'm not the one who asked to look! To save all this running back and forth, I should have brought a telescope with me!

As for observing women through a telescope, my uncle had a long history. There were all kinds of telescopes in his place—Zeiss, Olympus, and a Battery Commander bought from the former Soviet Union. He often leaned over the telescope, watching them for half an hour in the manner of Marshal Zhukov of the Soviet army. They say being under such surveillance frightens and bewilders you altogether. The girls in his neighborhood would often be so befuddled while walking that they would suddenly smack into lampposts. Later, they always used umbrellas when they went out, so my uncle couldn't see them from upstairs. Now my young aunt just lay there letting him look at her, with no umbrella, and my uncle didn't want to look. This is called not knowing when you have it good.

My uncle was depressed in the alkali field, but my younger aunt was just the opposite. After enjoying enough sunshine, she put on her boots, walked into the cold air, came over to my uncle and said, Convict Wang, you go get some sunshine too. Let me dig the alkali for a while. After saying this, she grabbed the pick and started digging. Meanwhile, my uncle lay down on the blue coat. If an alkali tractor was passing then at a distance, the people on the tractor would shout catcalls at her. This was because my young aunt had nothing on but a red silk scarf around her neck, a pair of sunglasses on her nose and goose bumps all over. There were quite a few tractors in the field, rolling around on the waste ground and jetting out dark smoke, like nineteenth-century steamboats. The sky was so blue in that place that it almost looked purple, the wind as cold as water, the alkali white and gleaming, and the air dry enough to turn skin into paper. My uncle shut his eyes, wanting to daydream in the sunshine—the defeated always like to daydream. He was thirty-eight at the time. He spread out his limbs and fell asleep.

After a while, my young aunt kicked him and said, Get up, Convict Wang. You won't be able to enjoy sunshine that way! You'll get a rash if you keep yourself so covered up. She referred to the way that my uncle slept fully dressed in the sunshine. Considering it was outdoors and in freezing temperatures, what she said was not particularly true. My young aunt bent over, dragging his pants all the way down to the shackles. If my uncle ever looked eight-yards tall, it was then. Then she bent over again, wildly unbuttoning the four buttons of his ragged coat and flinging it open. My uncle opened his eyes, and saw a red woman riding on his body with a red silk scarf around her neck and her hair flying like a wild horse's mane. He closed his eyes again. Although these actions had sexual overtones, they could also be interpreted as the instructor's concern for the prisoner—you can be sure the camp food was not very good. Letting him get some sunshine would provide him with additional vitamin D and prevent him from getting a calcium deficiency. After she finished, my young aunt dismounted from my uncle, seated herself beside him, pulled a pack of cigarettes out of her uniform pocket, and put one into her mouth. Just as she took out a windproof lighter and was about to light it, she changed her mind. She patted my uncle's chest with her palm and the lighter, and said, Stand up, Convict Wang! Don't you know the etiquette? On hearing her voice, my uncle stood up, leaned close to her and lit the cigarette for her. Later, every time my young aunt held a cigarette in her mouth, my uncle would reach out his hand, ask for the lighter and say, Reporting to the Instructor, now I know the etiquette!

Afterward, my uncle lay on the alkali flat with his limbs splayed. The wind blew and gathered up the broken bits of alkali, which dropped on his skin and burned as hot as sparks. The bits of white alkali chips disappeared in little red spots all over his body. My young aunt put the rest of a cigarette into his mouth and he continued to smoke after her. Then, she climbed on his body to make love to him, her hair and the scarlet silk scarf flying side by side. As my uncle breathed in and out, smoke came out of his nose and mouth. Later he raised his head to look down, and said, Reporting to the Instructor, do I need to put on a condom? But my young aunt said, You just lie there. Mind your own business. So he lay back, watching the clouds scatter in the sky. My young aunt patted his face; he turned around to look at her and asked, Reporting to the Instructor! Why did you pat my face?

My uncle had been a frivolous person. After living in the alkali field, he became serious and steady. This had something to do with the story's setting. It was a huge alkali flat, with a muddy, black sunken area in the center circled by a barbed wire fence. Inside that sunken area, there were dozens of rows of tents parted by a ditch in the middle, with water pipes lining the end of the ditch. At dusk, my uncle and the other inmates of the labor camp would wash their lunch pails there. The water from the pipes was alkaline, so the lunch pails were easy to clean. My uncle and aunt usually ate their meals inside their tent. It was a thick canvas tent with a lightbulb hanging in the center. My young aunt sat commandingly on the bedroll eating her meal, her legs forked and her head held upright; her box lunch contained white rice, hearts of cabbage, and a few pieces of sausage. My young uncle sat on a folding stool eating his meal, his legs crossed, his head lowered; his bowl contained stale rice and old cabbage, with no sausages at all. My young aunt grunted *moo,* and my uncle handed over his box. She gave him her sausages, and he took the box back, continuing to eat. Then my young aunt glared at him. She hurried to swallow the rice in her mouth and said, Convict Wang, don't you even say "thank you"? My uncle immediately responded, Yes, thanks! My aunt asked, Thank whom? My uncle hesitated a bit, and then said, Thank you, big sister! My young aunt fell into silence and the reason for that was because my uncle was fifteen years older than her. By the time they finished their meal, my aunt struck her box and said, Convict Wang! I think it would be better if you kept calling me "Instructor." My uncle agreed, took their boxes, and went out to wash them. My young aunt fell silent again. She felt very good, so good that her sides began shaking with laughter. She thought my uncle very amusing, herself amusing, too, and their life very enjoyable; on my uncle's side, he didn't think himself amusing, nor did he think my young aunt was, and to him this kind of life was a misery. Nevertheless, he still loved my young aunt because he had no other choice.

At this point, my uncle's story ended this way: when he came back from washing their lunch boxes, it was already dark and the wind had started blowing. He put their lunch boxes into a bag, hung it on the wall, and then fastened the door flap. The so-called door flap was just a canvas curtain with straps on the sides that could be tied to the tent. My uncle fastened every single strap and turned around, seeing my young aunt's uniform scattered over the ground. He picked the pieces up, folded them one by one, and then put them on a wooden shelf in a corner. After that, he stood in the middle of the tent at attention. At that point my young aunt had thrown herself under the quilt, face down, reading a book by a small table lamp. After a while, the lightbulb flickered a few times and went out, but my young aunt's table lamp was still on—it ran on batteries. She said, Convict Wang, it's time to go to bed! My uncle took off all of his clothes, including the shackles, which rusted during the day. But my uncle had a small wrench just right for unlocking shackles. After that he stood at attention, this time naked, trembling with the cold, while the tent shook in the wind. When his nose started running he couldn't help making a report, Reporting to the Instructor, I'm ready. My young aunt answered without turning around, Ready? Then just get in. Why the nonsense? My uncle tiptoed to the bedside, slipped under the covers, and snuggled up to my young aunt—there was only one set of blankets in the tent. Since my young aunt didn't have anything on, she gasped through her teeth when my uncle touched her. This made my uncle believe he should give her some room. But she said, Closer, you moron! After my young aunt finally finished the paragraph, she folded that page, switched off the light and turned her face toward my uncle, along with her breasts, lower abdomen, pubic hair, and so forth. She said, Convict Wang, hold me! Don't you have something to say? My uncle thought to himself: Well, it's dark. I'll say any crap as long as she doesn't handcuff me in the latrine again. So he said, Instructor, I love you! She said, Very good. What else? My uncle began to kiss her and their bodies tangled in the darkness. My young aunt enjoyed telling me these anecdotes very much, but I grew more anxious every time I heard her: the question of when my uncle got out, or whether he ever got out of that place, was all up to my aunt. If finally he could get out and learn to follow some rules, that wouldn't be too bad. But my young aunt said, "If he can't convince me that he loves me, he'll never get out of this place."

5

Now I can say that my uncle suffered injustice because of his painting. Just because no one understood his paintings, he was categorized as unfathomable. In the Qing dynasty, a poet wrote, "The cool breeze does not know words, why does it riffle through the pages?" This made people feel he was unfathomable, so the poet was taken to the execution ground and cut into pieces. Last century, a writer named Milan Kundera said: When a human being thinks, God laughs. This God is very unfathomable. Once I quoted this phrase from Kundera, and a leader overheard me. He said, We must denounce this God until he stinks! Afterward, he told me that he thought I was talking about someone named God. In a word, the charge against my uncle was "unfathomability." If he hadn't been unfathomable, he wouldn't have had all those troubles.

On the alkali field, the reason that my aunt kept my uncle and didn't want to release him was also because he was unfathomable. She told me that she met my uncle first in her math class. My uncle had started losing his hair after the IQ tests, and besides, he hadn't found any quick way to get out of there. Because of these two things he was in a bad mood, and the hair on the back of his head stood up like a hedgehog's. In the class, he glared, gnashed his teeth hard, and often bit off his pencil and ate it as if it were a stick of candy. Then he would wipe the graphite bits left at the corner of his mouth and smear his whole mouth black. He ate all seven of the pencils he got for each class. My young aunt thought he looked scary and often reminded him, Convict Wang, I'm not the one who took your permit away, why stare at me like that? My uncle snapped awake as if from a dream. He stood up and answered, I'm sorry, Instructor! You're very pretty. I love you. The last line just occurred to him at that very moment. My uncle always had a well-oiled tongue and couldn't change even after he went to the Art Reeducation Institute. I told my young aunt that she was truly very pretty. She said, Yeah, yeah. Then she laughed, I'm pretty. But it wasn't his place to say so. Later she told me that although she was still young, she was already a wily veteran. At the Art Reeducation Institute, whenever a student complimented an instructor's looks, he'd have something on his mind. As for saying he loved her, he should have been punished for that. I never saw my young aunt hit my uncle but from their expressions it most probably had happened.

My young aunt also said that in the Art Reeducation Institute, bored students often tried to butter her up. She always struck them after she heard that sort of talk. For some reason my uncle seemed different from those others. These two were destined to be together. The evidence of their destiny was that when she looked at his paintings, she felt unfathomable and very horny. Once, the three of us, my uncle, my aunt, and I, lay on the alkali flat. My young aunt was on her belly sunbathing, on a plastic sheet; my uncle lay there with all his clothes on, like a corpse, except his eyes were wide open, focusing on his nose. My aunt's naked body was very beautiful, but I didn't risk looking at her. I was afraid that my uncle might get jealous. He looked terrible. I wanted to comfort him, but didn't dare, for my young aunt might accuse us of conspiracy. What a strange situation to be dragged into! Just imagining it would be strange.

My young aunt said she liked my uncle's paintings. The Art Reeducation Institute had gotten some from Lijiakou police station. But those paintings took up too much space, so the institute decided to throw them into the garbage. My young aunt asked for all of them and stored them in her dorm. When nobody was around, she would look at them. Therefore, it was not by chance that my young aunt escorted my uncle to the alkali field. As the saying goes: Better to have a thief steal from you than keep you in mind. My young aunt had kept my young uncle in mind for a long time. That's my conclusion, but my young aunt had a different opinion. She said: It was the god of art, Apollo, who brought us together. At this point, she nudged my uncle and asked: Is the god of art Apollo? My uncle responded, I don't know who he is. His voice was low and deep, sounding like my dead cousin come back to life.

I often visited the alkali field, and every time, I would tell my young aunt that my uncle loved her. After my young aunt heard this, her eyes would turn golden and she would say, He loves me? Fine! Then she would burst out laughing, which made me doubt whether she really considered it fine. Otherwise, she wouldn't have laughed like that. If it were another woman, how she felt wouldn't matter. But my young aunt had my uncle's life in her hands and I believed it was my responsibility to make her feel good. So I tried to approach her in another way, If my young uncle didn't really love you, how would you feel? She said, He doesn't really love me? That's also fine! Then she laughed again, with what to me seemed like a ferocious grin. We had deadlocked over this issue, so it was time for me to try something else.

One time, I brought all kinds of newspaper clippings to my uncle—the Japanese had taken my uncle's paintings to Paris and arranged a show for him, which caused a sensation. The show was called "2010—W2" and didn't reveal the painter's identity, which was one of the reasons for the sensation. All the newspapers agreed that the visual effect of this set of paintings was amazing; as to whether they were great works, only a few thought so. At the entrance to the exhibit, a painting looking like a crazy donkey dominated the entire show. Even someone with a good inner ear would feel dizzy after looking at it for five seconds. It happened that one person in the audience had Ménière's syndrome. When he looked at this painting, he felt sky and earth spin to the right while his body fell to the left—a jack couldn't have kept him up. So he was led to another painting that looked like a crazy horse and then felt the sky and earth spin to the left, so he finally managed to stand straight. Then he turned back and went home; for three days, he could eat nothing and drink only a little ice water. In the center of the exhibit hall a painting hung, which after viewing, people would feel all the blood had rushed to their head. Whether you were a man or a woman, old or young, your hair would stand up, with the exception of men with crew cuts. Blonde beauties with hair down to their shoulders soon looked like clowns with pointy hats. At the same time, audience members' eyes turned upward, showing the whites. A man with arteriosclerosis immediately had a stroke. Another painting made people feel that all their internal organs were traveling downward; young men with straight backs would become stoop shouldered, and men with hernias would feel like they had a hot water bottle hanging from their crotches. People made all kinds of guesses about the identity of the artist named "W2," some religious leaders had already decided to label him a blasphemer, a minion of Satan, and had ordered his execution. They killed some Williams, Webers, and Willises, and were trying to kill the people who could paint in the World Health Organization (WHO), and even made West Point change its name. At the time none of them got the idea of killing all the Chinese with the surname of Wang. There're one hundred million people named Wang in China, the equivalent of the population of a large country. I don't think they would dare risk it. I showed these clippings to my young aunt, trying to make her understand that my uncle was a great artist and she should treat him well. My young aunt said, Great! Great! If he weren't great, would I be in charge of him? Later, as I was leaving, my uncle took the opportunity to kick me. He used this method to communicate to me that advertising his greatness to my young aunt wasn't good for him. This was the last time that he kicked me. Afterward, he was sick as a dog and hadn't the strength to kick me anymore.

While I obsessed over saving my uncle, he slowly languished in the alkali field. His lips protruded and his cheek became as hollow as a monkey's. My young aunt also worried and asked me to bring some canned food from town, especially five-kilogram cans of lunch meat. I put them into plastic string bags and hung them on my neck, one on each side, very silly looking. On the bus to the alkali field, people said I looked like Pigsy* with a sword strapped on—a slob of a soldier. This lunch meat was mostly used by restaurants in cold dishes, with the meat cut into small pieces; if you ate big chunks, it was very greasy and hard to swallow. As my young aunt opened the can in the tent, my uncle lay beside her and began to throw up. She scooped a piece of the meat and forced it into my uncle's mouth. Then she hurried to toss the spoon aside, pressed my uncle's mouth with one hand and choked his neck with the other hand. She gazed into his eyes and said, One, two, three! Swallow! By the time she finished stuffing my uncle, my young aunt was drenched in sweat. She wiped her hands and said, You, boy, go find out where they sell those machines to force-feed ducks. By then my uncle's lips had swollen and really did look like a duck's bill.

---

* Pigsy is a mythological character from the famous Chinese novel *Journey to the West*, written by Wu Chengen in the sixteenth century.

Since he didn't eat well in the alkali field and also felt depressed, my uncle suffered from impotence. But my aunt knew what to do. These anecdotes of my uncle's he told me himself little by little and somewhat shyly. My aunt added a lot: When he lay on the alkali flat, the thing slouched limply, like a steamed taro. You'd have to shout at him: Attention! Then he would stand up, like a prairie dog, poking his head out and looking around. Of course, you couldn't yell at him unless you were my young aunt. The thing was very good at following orders. He could not only understand "attention" and "at ease," but also knew "right face" or "left face," and "forward march," et cetera. By contrast, my uncle had problems following orders. He couldn't tell left from right; if you told him "turn left," he would surely turn right; when he marched, he would swing the wrong arm. But the thing didn't have any of these problems. My young aunt would laugh whenever mentioning this, saying that his IQ was higher than my uncle's. If my uncle's IQ were 50, his would be 150, three times higher. For a genital organ, the score was pretty unusual. My aunt was teaching him math, but he hadn't mastered it yet. So far, he only knew to nod twice when asked what one plus one equaled. But my young aunt was very confident about his talent for mathematics and resolved to teach him calculus. She had been teaching my uncle the subject but he hadn't mastered it. She also described in detail how after she gave the order "attention" the little guy staggered up, turned to an exclamation mark from a question mark, and brightened his color from dark gray to scarlet, like an American apple. She said that any woman would feel overcome at the sight. But I thought men would feel the same way.

My young aunt also said: An artist is indeed an artist, even his tool is different from others'—other men definitely don't have this talent. My uncle blushed at hearing this, and he said, Reporting to the Instructor, please don't insult me. You can shoot a soldier but don't shame him. But my aunt just shrugged and made light of the subject, Cut the nonsense! Why would I kill you? Come here, give me a kiss. My uncle had to contain his boiling anger and kiss my young aunt. After the kiss, he forgot about the insult. In my opinion, my uncle didn't have the dash he used to have, and had become a little dull, at least around my aunt. I heard that if my aunt shouted "Attention!" at him, he would ask foolishly, Who? My aunt said, "At ease!" He would also ask who should be at ease. In the tent, my aunt lowered her voice and said, Comrade, you went the wrong way. . . . My uncle would look blank for a moment and ask: Were you talking to me? Did I commit an error? My young aunt mocked him: A human talks to you and you answer like a dog. Sometimes, she talked to my uncle and he made no response at all. She had to pat his face and he would say something like, Sorry, Instructor. I didn't know you were talking to me. The disturbing part was that my uncle and that thing of his were both named Wang Er. My young aunt was confused too and said, The two of you together will be the death of me! After a while, my uncle didn't know how many selves he had.

My uncle and my aunt reached an impasse in the alkali field. I thought there were two reasons for it at the time. The first was because my young aunt didn't understand art; she only knew how to make fun of artists. If I had known what art was and could have explained it to her in a few sentences, she would probably have let my uncle leave. Since I was unable to, my uncle couldn't get out.

When I first got to college, I was so occupied with the true meaning of art that I constantly forgot about east-west-south-north. People would see me circle around the sports field; if someone tried counting the circles, he'd lose track and walk away. I thought and thought, and then I forgot sunrise and sunset. People would see me sitting on the roof, smoking at midnight, throwing down cigarette butts one after another—the incredible part about my sitting that high was that I had acrophobia. Girls fell in love with me because of this, saying I reminded them of Wittgenstein. But I always told them: Wittgenstein is nobody! After hearing this, they loved me more. But I was too busy solving this difficult problem to fall in love with any of them, letting them fly away from me one after another. Thinking back on this now, I can't help feeling regret, because some of them were very smart; some were very pretty; others were smart and pretty, which was more unusual. As for the true meaning of art, it's why people want to paint, and write poetry and fiction. I believed that as an artist, I first had to think it out clearly. Unfortunately, to this day I still haven't figured out the answer.

I still miss the time I was a freshman at the university. Back then I worked on a physics paper; prepared for the entrance exam for the graduate program in history; visited my uncle from time to time; constantly pondered the true meaning of art; participated in all the discussions on any of the trendy topics in Beijing; and managed to steal some leisure time from my busy schedule to go after a pretty girl in the biology department. During the height of summer, this girl would comb her long hair into a ponytail and wear a white T-shirt and striped culottes; droplets of sweat would often form on her neck and behind her ears. When I met her on campus, I would invite her to go to the pinewoods with me. She would carefully put a handkerchief over the pine needles, sit on it, and take off her leather sandals and knee socks. By then I would get absentminded, forgetting my intention to use my nose to sniff the sour smell around her neck—the girls all agreed that I had a lovely nose, warm in winter and cool in summer. That was why she didn't mind lifting her ponytail to let me smell the soft hair on the nape of her neck. From this angle, the girl smelled like cheese. Unfortunately, I'd often remember that I had something else to do, so I'd remove my nose from her neck and leave in a hurry. I remember once I detected a heavy scent of something from her breasts. Before I could tell what it was, suddenly I remembered that I had to catch the bus to see my uncle; I hurried away. Next time I saw her, she looked like she was about to cry and threw the dish she was carrying into my face. The dish contained a half portion of garlic stalk and a half portion of tofu, plus several ounces of rice. The garlic stalk was overcooked, too soft; the tofu was cooked with five-spice powder that had gone bad, a little bitter; the rice was steamed in a stainless-steel tray and then cut into four portions. I hate for rice to be cooked this way. From this incident, I learned about her bad temper and some other things that I didn't like. So I stopped thinking of her, except for occasionally thinking that she might still be thinking of me.

On the alkali flat, when I was considering how to save my uncle, it suddenly dawned on me that the truth of art was unfathomability. However, this answer meant nothing, for nobody in the world knew what unfathomability was. If anyone knew, it wouldn't be unfathomability.

Another reason that my uncle was trapped in the alkali field was that he was not good at love. If he had been good at it, he would have been able to get my aunt to release him. In my opinion, love was a kind of athletics; some people could run a hundred yards in ten seconds, and others needed twenty seconds to finish the same distance. Many of the people who went to the Art Reeducation Institute at the same time as my uncle were already out, strolling the streets holding their former instructors' arms; it seemed they were better at love than my uncle. The secret of athletics is practice. So I started to practice, not to save my uncle, but to save myself in the future.

Recently, I met a woman at our class reunion. She said she remembered me, and her memory of me was poetic. First, she remembered a wind at the beginning of this century, full of yellow dust. Below the yellow dust, the leaves appeared unusually green. Between the yellow and the green was a boy, wrapped in dusty corduroy clothes, languidly walking across the sports field as if sick—the boy was me—though I was never sick at the university. I didn't know why she said I looked sick. But judging by what she said, it would have been the period before I started visiting the alkali field.

This woman is my colleague, now living overseas; she smelled like glacial acetic acid from a bottle, almost like an acid bomb. In her poetic reminiscence, the most memorable thing about those yellow-dust days was the leaves dripping with green, the leaves symbolizing sex. Then she mentioned a small room and a window. The window was associated with a mathematical expression—the expression was two times two, which signified the four panes of glass in the window; square, covered by a piece of cloth with a black and red pattern. The wind ballooned the piece of patterned clothes above a wrinkled, narrow bed; an indigo batiked sheet was spread over the bed. She lay naked on the sheet and tried very hard to stretch her body; in other words, she tried to make her head and her toes separate as far from each other as possible; so her belly sank back into the sheet. Her legs shined with a gray luster. A smell permeated this strange scene, something fishy; in other words, the smell of fresh semen. If you'd told me this smell had something to do with me, I'd have been really surprised. But the room was the dormitory I lived in as a sophomore, and I lived there alone. As for what I did there, I don't remember anything at all.

This woman applied heavy eye shadow, dyed her hair dirty blonde, and now weighed about three hundred pounds. It was very difficult for me to associate her with any girl I had known in the past. Since she knew my room, and even my smell, I couldn't deny our relationship. She also said, at the time we were together, I was a quiet, tense-faced person, often seeming to have something in mind; then all of a sudden, my semen would start jetting, warm as pee. Because I was such an absentminded bed wetter, she missed me all the time. But I didn't remember having wet my bed; besides, if you called this love—I would definitely deny it.

At the university, there was a time I took classes like a lunatic, twenty courses one semester. I couldn't attend every class, so I asked my classmates to bring walkie-talkies with them. I myself sat in the dorm, keeping track of the lectures through different earphones. My room looked like a switchboard, and my face got pale. The professors in my department suspected me of taking heroin and urged me to have a blood test. After finding out that I wasn't a drug addict, they admonished me: Why the hurry to graduate? The most important thing is to be a good student. But I was busy taking finals first, and then busy taking makeups. When I went to take the medical Latin makeup, I looked like a dead person, and the professor let me pass without asking me a thing. Then I collapsed to the ground and was taken to the school hospital. It was my young uncle's situation that drove me so crazy. Whenever I thought about his predicament, it felt like hundreds of claws scratching at my heart.

During winter vacation, I heard that a girl in the chemistry department had taken twenty-one courses, one more than I did. I fell in love with her because of this, waiting for her in front of her dorm every day with a bouquet. She was a small girl with thick glasses, but the eyes behind the glasses were very large, two Archimedean curves rounding into circles. She had a pale face and a pair of hands like bird's claws, and was a little hunchbacked, too. Later on, I discovered her breasts flat against her chest, no bigger than mine, just a pair of nipples; her shoulders were as thin as mine when I was thirteen. To sum things up, in terms of the parts above her navel and below her knees, she was completely a boy. About things between men and women, she had an academic interest, always asking: Why is it like this? I told her that I loved her and didn't want to love anybody else in this life. She pushed up her glasses and said: Why do you want to love me? Why don't you want to love somebody else in this life? I couldn't come up with an answer, so I suggested we make love. As she said afterward, making love didn't solve the problem. If I really had loved her, I wouldn't have needed a reason. But things without reasons make people suspicious. Therefore she came to the conclusion that whoever told her he loved her would make her suspicious. After she said what she did, I felt like I didn't really love her. She listened and then pushed up her glasses and said: Why don't you love me anymore? Then without thinking it through I fell in love with her again. We seesawed like this. A semester later, her body suddenly began to develop. She bought a pair of contact lenses, turned into a slender beauty and a dumbbell also. By then there were many pursuers gathering around her and I had lost interest.

6

Once, my uncle, aunt, and I sunbathed till dusk. At dusk, my young aunt stood up and looked around. The sunset's red and white colors shone on her body, making her look like a goddess. If I wanted to go into detail, I would say her shoulders reflected like mirrors, and her breasts cast a shadow on her chest. On her flat belly, there was a clump of hair, like a squirrel's tail—I suspect as her nephew I shouldn't be describing her this way—then she bent over to put on her pants, and I had to get back to school. It was the only time that I saw my young aunt in the nude. I never had another chance. If I had known that, I would have taken a good look at her then.

After talking about my young aunt, I should say something about my young uncle. His case was redressed later; the court announced his innocence, and the Art Reeducation Institute declared him a good student. The Oil Painting Association restored his membership and his permit and even wanted to put him on the Directorate of the Fine Arts Association. But my young uncle didn't collect his permit, nor did he want to join the Oil Painting Association. So the authorities concerned decided to dismiss my young uncle and revoke his painting permit on the charge of not having the good sense to appreciate when someone is doing him a favor. However, my young aunt objected to their decision and wanted to sue. Her argument was that since my uncle neither rejoined the Fine Arts Association nor collected his permit, how was it possible to dismiss him and cancel his permit? But she lost the lawsuit. The court ruled that as the authority in the painting field, the Oil Painting Association could revoke anyone's membership or cancel his permit, whether he was a member or not, or a painter or not. After the ruling, the Oil Painting Association called a meeting and solemnly decided to dismiss my young aunt. From then on, she could write, but it would be illegal for her to paint. Now, neither my uncle nor my aunt had a permit. Anyhow, he continued painting and selling his paintings to that Japanese. But the price had gone down a lot. The Japanese guy said that with the world economy in a slump, paintings weren't easy to unload. Actually it was a lie. The truth was that my young uncle's reputation had declined—he'd fallen a little out of fashion.

After talking about my uncle, now I should say something about the Japanese—the guy had aged, white stubble grew around his mouth. When I stopped at a red light at an intersection, he'd strut down the crosswalk, open the door of my car, and say, Mr. Wang, paintings! And he took off with the paintings. By the way, my old uncle is called Wang Da, and my young uncle is Wang Er. My mother was such a strong-willed woman that I had no choice but to adopt her last name of "Wang." My young uncle stored those paintings at my place. If the red light were fairly long, the Japanese would chat with me some more. He said that he really missed my young uncle and wanted to see him sometime. I lied to him, My uncle has left to become a nun. He can't break the rules of the order and come out to see you. Put him out of your mind. He corrected me, Monk, you mean monk. Then he closed the door, bowed to me and walked away. Actually, he knew I was lying. If he hadn't contacted my uncle, how would he find me? On the other hand, I also knew the Japanese was lying. We all lied, nobody trusted anyone else.

Somebody said that the Japanese was actually Brazilian; many people of Japanese descent lived in Brazil. He had a black wife, dark as ink. Once he brought her to China. She wore a green cheongsam while taking a walk with him, which led to a misunderstanding. The police arrested her under the impression she was my young uncle. In the police station, they dipped a towel into water, gasoline, and acetone, and scrubbed her face hard. What came off was not black greasepaint, but blood. By the time people from the Brazilian embassy got word and rushed over, the sign over the station had been changed to Daycare Center; all the policemen wore white uniforms and pretended to be washing the black woman's face. She was about six foot six, almost as tall as a lamppost. The claim that she was a lost child seemed dubious. The Japanese fellow also had a white mistress, white as snow. Once when they walked on the street, there was a mix-up again. The policemen took her to the station. The first sentence they said was, Hey! Wang Er, very realistic! How much bleaching powder did you use? Then they pinched her nose, trying to find out if it was plaster, which made her tears pour down like rain; they pulled her hair hard, suspecting it was a wig, and soon her blonde hair looked like a hornet's nest. When the employees from the embassy arrived, the sign over the police station was changed to Beauty Salon. But it was a little strange for a beauty salon to make her nose look like a drunkard's and her hair like a naval mine. Later, whenever they walked on the street with the Japanese guy, those foreign women would hang a sign around their necks, which read: "I am not Wang Er."

One day, a policeman seized me, grabbing my tie and dragging me off the ground. Then he said cheerfully, Great, Wang Er, now you don't even try to disguise yourself. I said calmly, Big uncle, you're making a mistake. I'm not Wang Er. I'm his nephew. He stared at me blankly, then put me down and let out a gob of spit, which landed on my leather shoes. He thought for a while, then smoothed my tie, wiped my leather shoes, saluted me, and pretended to walk away. Actually, he didn't walk away but stealthily followed me. Every ten minutes he would rush in front of me and take my pulse, to see if it was racing. I was calm every time, so he didn't dare grab me again. Fortunately he didn't take me to the police station, otherwise, when the people from my work unit came to get me, the police would have had to switch signs: Judo Studio. The reason that these things happened was because they knew my uncle was still selling his paintings in secret. They really wanted to arrest him, but couldn't catch him. That was not important—the important thing was when they grabbed me, I felt excited and got an erection, which meant that like my young uncle, I had the artistic gift. This probably was beyond question.

So far, I've talked about everyone except me. When I was a little kid, I wanted to be an artist. After witnessing my young uncle's fate, I changed my mind and began to try other things, including working as an attendant at a public toilet. The one I kept watch over was a dark green building that looked like it was built of glazed bricks, but actually was molded concrete, with a layer of veneer glued to the surface to simulate glaze. Rain showers made it peel so badly that it looked like a turtle with ringworm. There were plenty of long, narrow mirrors inside. Peering at yourself in the mirror, you would feel like you were in a cage. The room smelled of bitter almond, a kind of disinfectant. I stood by the door, distributing bathroom tissue to people. Once in a while I had to clean the inside with a fire hose, turning the people who were sitting on the toilets into drowned rats. One thing I'll never forget was when I asked for tips; if a customer forgot to give me money, I would grab his clothes, and even tear off his pocket. After a while nobody dared not to tip me. I soon got fired because I worked too diligently.

Another time I set up a stall in front of the railway station, repairing watches and lighters. Like other repair stalls, mine was also a glass box, which could be pushed away. Because of the greenhouse effect, it was very hot to sit inside, and I sweated a lot and was thirsty all the time. The watches I fixed wouldn't keep time, but could light cigarettes; the lighters worked as watches, but couldn't strike a light. My customers weren't very satisfied. Another time I wore sunglasses, pretended to be blind, and made a living by singing on the street. Very few people gave me money. For a blind person, my clothes were not dirty enough. They also said my singing was so terrible that I could make children pee faster. Later on, I tried baby-sitting, singing for kids. They couldn't pee at all after hearing my singing. When their parents came home, they would say: Mommy, this uncle sang. Then they began to cry uncontrollably. I tried all kinds of jobs in order to keep stalling and avoid my fate.

Finally I grew up and got a job in the writing department; my uncle also came out of the alkali field and married my young aunt. He still paints. It is my young aunt who changed jobs, working in public relations at a big company. This proves that my uncle and I have no other talents besides painting and palaver, respectively. My young aunt, however, had many talents. Sometimes she called me in the middle of the night to complain about my uncle, saying that all my uncle knew was how to play mysterious little tricks in his painting. He had exhausted his talent and couldn't create the kind of paintings that made people dizzy anymore; she also said that one part of his body worked in the old way, she had to give orders to him every day and pretended to like that very much—but she was bored to death. This seems to imply that she got a raw deal by marrying my uncle. But after every conversation, she would always add: Don't tell your uncle what I said. If you dare reveal any bit of it, I'll kill you. As for me, I write stories every day. To tell the truth, I don't even know what I'm writing.

For all we face today, I bear the responsibility. That day, when I returned from the alkali field, I was worried and upset. So I played with my computer, trying to find a game on the Internet. After searching here and there, I didn't find a game, but I came across an electronic magazine called *Physics Today*. Though I majored in physics, I never read anything in physics except textbooks. That day was an exception. The magazine's banner headline read: Who is the greatest painter after Dali—W2 or 486? W2 was my uncle's alias, 486 was a personal computer at the end of the last century, completely obsolete nowadays. You can buy five or six of them for just a dollar. There was an illustration in the article, showing a 486 computer with the hernia-inducing painting of my uncle's on the screen. Of course, it was only a picture of a picture so you wouldn't get a hernia, although it still made you want to shit. After you finished the article, you didn't even want to shit anymore. The article mentioned that at the end of the last century, people began to study physical processes from disorder to order, also known as "chaos." In computer simulation, chaos looks very pretty on the screen. The most famous representations are the Mandelbrot sets, which, magnified, look like the tail of a sea horse and which I believe everyone has seen. By the way, the Mandelbrot sets don't make people dizzy and have nothing in common with my young uncle's paintings. But the article's author invented a formula called Yi Ya Ah La, which uses an obsolete 486 computer to paint and can make people much dizzier than ever. Simply put, a formula plus a junk computer that is cheaper than a box of matches can make paintings like my uncle's. Once you know this you're not going to get dizzy or have a hernia at my uncle's paintings. Obviously, after learning this, my young aunt wouldn't get horny anymore when she looked at my uncle's paintings. This article gave me a different feeling about my young uncle, young aunt, art, love, as well as the whole world, which is: you open your asshole to fart and nothing much comes out. If I hadn't surfed the net for games, everything would have stayed the same: my young uncle still as unfathomable as before, and my young aunt still obsessed with him. I am not a boy anymore, why do I still play games?

After reading the article, I hesitated for a long time and finally made up my mind. I made a hundred copies of the article, attached a letter asking redress for my uncle's case, and sent it to all the departments concerned—after all, my uncle was suffering and I couldn't sit there without lending him a helping hand. The department concerned responded immediately: my young uncle wasn't unfathomable. What he painted were Yi Ya Ah La sets. Why are we keeping him in prison—Let him go! With this news, I sped to the alkali field and told my young uncle and aunt everything. My young aunt let out a long sigh after she heard this, and said, So that's what they are! I'm sorry, Convict Wang, you've suffered a lot! I'll ask the Institute to pay you some compensation after I get back. You don't have to keep saying you love me anymore. When my young uncle heard my words, he fell to the ground like a dead person; but as soon as he heard those words of my aunt, he came back to life, rose from the ground and said, Reporting to the Instructor, I really love you. I was never using you! Et cetera. After my young aunt heard this, her eyes turned a golden color. She grinned at me, Did you hear that? Let's beat this death-before-dishonor guy! But before we could start she changed her mind and heaved a long sigh, Never mind. Don't beat him, looks like he really has fallen in love with me. This seems to imply that if my uncle continued to be unfathomable, it would have been impossible for him to fall in love with my young aunt and she would have had to beat him hard for that reason, but it would also be very enjoyable to make love to him; if he were no longer unfathomable, though he could fall in love with my young aunt, and she couldn't beat him from then on, it would also be very boring to make love to him. My young aunt and uncle left the alkali field, got married, and lived their life; everything became ordinary and predictable.

The year is 2015. I'm a writer. I still think about the true meaning of art. What is it anyway?

The Golden Age

1

At twenty-one, I was placed in a production team for reeducation in Yunnan. That year Chen Qingyang was twenty-six and a doctor who happened to work where I did. I was on the fourteenth production team down the mountain, and she was on the fifteenth team up the mountain. One day she came down the mountain to see me, to discuss the fact that she was not damaged goods. I didn't know her too well at the time, barely you might say. The issue she wanted to discuss was this: Despite the fact that everyone believed she was damaged goods, she didn't think she was. Because, to be damaged goods she had to have cheated on her husband, but she never did. Although her husband had been in prison for a year, she hadn't slept with another man, nor had she ever done anything like that. Therefore she simply couldn't understand why people kept calling her damaged goods. If I'd wanted to comfort her, it wouldn't have been hard; I could prove logically that she was not damaged goods. If Chen Qingyang were damaged goods, she would have had to have cheated on her husband, and therefore, there must be a man with whom she'd cheated. Since at present no one could point out such a man, the proposition that Chen Qingyang had slept with another man was untenable. Yet I insisted on saying that Chen Qingyang was damaged goods, and that this was beyond question.

Chen Qingyang came to me to ask me to prove she wasn't damaged goods because I had come to her for a shot. The whole thing unfolded as follows: During the farm's busy season our team leader would not assign me to plow fields. Instead he made me plant rice seedlings so that I could not stand straight most of the time. Anyone familiar with me knew about the injury to my lower back, not to mention that I was a tall man, over six feet. Having worked like this for a month, the pain in my lower back became so intolerable that I couldn't fall asleep without steroid injections. The clinic at our team had a bunch of needles whose coating had completely peeled off, with tips all bent like fish-hooks, which often pulled flesh from my lower back. After a while my waist looked like it had been peppered by a shotgun, and the scars didn't fade for a long time. Under the circumstances, I recalled that the doctor at the fifteenth team, Chen Qingyang, had graduated from Beijing Medical School. Maybe she would be able to tell the difference between a hypodermic and a crotchet needle. So I went to see her. Not half an hour after my visit, she chased after me to my room, wanting me to prove that she wasn't damaged goods.

Chen Qingyang said she didn't look down on damaged goods at all. In fact, from what she observed, damaged goods seemed to have soft hearts, loved to help others and, most of all, hated to disappoint people. Therefore, she even had a sneaking admiration for people like them. However, the problem was not whether damaged goods were good or not good, but lay in the fact that she was not damaged goods at all, just as a cat was not a dog. If a cat were called a dog, it wouldn't feel comfortable. Now everyone called her damaged goods, which drove her to distraction and made her almost forget who she was.

As Chen Qingyang sat in my thatched shack and poured out her troubles, she had on a white smock that left her arms and legs exposed, the same outfit she had worn earlier in her clinic. The only differences were that she had tied back her long, loose hair with a handkerchief and put on a pair of sandals. As I looked at her, I began to wonder what was under her white smock, whether she had something on—or nothing at all, which would show what a beautiful woman Chen Qingyang was because she believed that it didn't really matter whether or not she wore underwear. That kind of confidence needs to have been built up from childhood. I told her that she was definitely damaged goods, and even enumerated several reasons to convince her. I said that so-called damaged goods was just a denotation. If people say you're damaged goods, then you must be damaged goods—there isn't much logic to it; if people say you slept with another man, you must have done it—there is not much logic to that either. As for why they say you're damaged goods, in my opinion it's because of this: People generally agree that if a married woman hasn't cheated on her husband, her face must be leathery, and her breasts must sag. Now your face is not dark but fair, your breasts are not hanging down but jutting out, so you must be damaged goods. If you don't want to be damaged goods, you should try to darken your face and make your breasts sag so people won't accuse you of being damaged goods, which, of course, is a raw deal for you. If you don't want a raw deal, sleep with another man so you can think of yourself as damaged goods, too. Other people are not obliged to find out if you are damaged goods before calling you that, but you are obliged to stop them from calling you damaged goods. As Chen Qingyang listened to my words, her face flushed and her eyes widened with anger. She looked like she was about to slap me. This woman was famous for her slapping; many men had felt her slaps. However, suddenly disheartened, she said, "All right, let me be damaged goods. As far as drooping or not drooping, dark or not dark, that's none of your business." She also said that if I spent too much time pondering these matters, I would very likely get slapped.

Imagine the scene twenty years ago, when Chen Qingyang and I discussed the damaged goods issue. Back then, my face was baked brown, my lips were dry and chapped, with bits of paper and tobacco stuck to them, my hair was matted like a coconut husk, the many holes in the ragged army greatcoat I wore were patched with bandages, as I sat, legs crossed, on the wooden bed, looking like a total hooligan. You can imagine when Chen Qingyang heard such a person talking about whether her breasts drooped or not, how the palm of her hand itched. She was a little oversensitive, but that was because many strong men went to see her who weren't sick at all. What they wanted to see was damaged goods, not a doctor. I was the only exception. My lower back looked like it had been struck by Pigsy's rake. Whether my back really hurt or not, those holes alone would justify my visit to the doctor. Those holes also made her hope she might be able to convince me she was not damaged goods. Even if there were just one person who believed she wasn't damaged goods, it would be very different than no one believing her. But I intentionally disappointed her.

This is what I thought: if I wanted to prove she was not damaged goods and I could, then things would be too easy. The truth was I couldn't prove anything, except things that didn't need proving. In spring, our team leader claimed I was the one who had shot out the left eye of his dog, which was why the dog always looked at people with its head tilted, as if she were dancing ballet. From then on, he always gave me a hard time. Three things could have proved my innocence:

1. The team leader had no dog;
2. The dog was born blind in the left eye;
3. I'm a man with no hands who can't aim a gun.

Finally, none of the three requirements could be established: the team leader did have a brown dog; her left eye was indeed blinded by a shot; I could not only aim a gun but was also was an excellent marksman. To make matters worse, I'd borrowed an air rifle from Luo Xiaosi not long before the incident, and using a bowl of mung beans as bullets, killed a couple of pounds of mice in an empty granary. Of course, there were other crack shots on our production team, and one of them was Luo Xiaosi. When he fired at the team leader's dog, I stood right beside him watching. But I couldn't inform on other people, and my relationship with Luo Xiaosi was not bad. Besides, if the team leader could have handled Luo Xiaosi, he wouldn't have accused me. So I kept quiet. To keep silent meant to acquiesce. That was why in the spring I had to plant rice seedlings, stooped over in the field like a broken electricity pole; in the autumn I had to herd cattle, so I couldn't get a hot meal. Of course, I could not take this lying down. One day as I walked on the mountain, the team leader's dog came into view. I happened to have Luo Xiaosi's air rifle with me, so I fired a bullet and blinded her right eye. With neither left eye nor right eye, the dog couldn't get back to the team leader's house—God knows where she went.

I remember in those days, besides herding cattle on the mountain and lying in bed, I didn't have anything to do and nothing seemed to matter. But Chen Qingyang came down the mountain again to see me. There was another rumor in the air that she was having an affair with me and this time she wanted me to prove our innocence. I told her that we would have to prove two things first before our innocence could be established:

1. Chen Qingyang was a virgin;
2. Castrated at birth, I was unable to have sex.

These two things would be hard to prove, so we couldn't prove our innocence. I preferred to prove our guilt. On hearing my words, Chen Qingyang's face first turned pale and then blushed all over. Finally she stood up and left without saying a word.

Chen Qingyang told me later that I had always been a scoundrel. The first time she wanted me to prove her innocence, I looked up at the ceiling and began to talk nonsense; the next time she wanted me to prove our innocence, I earnestly suggested having intercourse with her. So she decided she was going to slap me sooner or later. If I had guessed her plan at the time, the things that happened later might never have happened.

2

On my twenty-first birthday, I was herding buffalo at the riverside. In the afternoon I fell asleep on the grass. I remembered covering myself with a few banana leaves before I fell asleep, but by the time I woke up I found nothing on my body. (Perhaps the buffalo had eaten the leaves.) The sunshine in the subtropical dry season had burned my entire body red, leaving me in an agony of burning and itching. My little Buddha pointed to the sky like an arrow, bigger than ever. That was how I spent my birthday.

When I woke up, the sun glared down on me from a frighteningly blue sky. A layer of fine dust, like a coating of talcum powder, covered my whole body. I'd experienced numerous erections in my life, but none as vigorous and magnificent as that time. Perhaps it was because of the location, so isolated from the villages that not even a soul could be seen.

I got up to check on my buffalo, only to find them all crouching at the far fork of the rivers, chewing grass quietly. It was a surpassingly still moment, and the white wind was gently blowing across the field. On the bank, several pairs of bulls from the mountain village were fighting each other. Their eyes had turned red, and saliva drooled from the corner of their mouths. This sort of bull had tightly packed balls and protruding penises. Our bulls were not like that. They would lie on the ground and stay put no matter how hard the other bulls tried to provoke them. To prevent our bulls from hurting each other and slowing down the spring plowing, we castrated all of them.

I was present every time they castrated the bulls. Ordinary bulls could just be cut with a knife. But for extremely wild ones, you have to employ the art of hammer-smashing, which is to cut open their scrotums, take out the balls, and then use a wooden hammer to pulverize them. From then on these altered bulls knew nothing but grazing and working. No need to tie them down if you wanted to kill them. Our team leader, the one who always wielded the hammer, had no doubts that surgery of this kind would also work on humans. He would shout at us all the time: You young bulls! You need a good hammering to make you behave. In his way of thinking, this red, stiff, foot-long thing on my body was the incarnation of evil.

Of course, I had a different opinion. To me, the thing was extremely important, as important as my existence itself. The darkness began to settle in, and a cloud drifted idly across the sky. The lower half of the cloud was immersed in darkness and the upper half still floated in sunshine. That day I was twenty-one, and in the golden age of my life. I had so many desires; I wanted to love, to eat, and to be turned in a flash into the half-bright and half-dark cloud in the sky. Only much later did I realize that life is a slow process of being hammered. People grow old day after day, their desire disappears little by little, and finally they become like those hammered bulls. However, that idea never crossed my mind on my twenty-first birthday. I thought I would always be lively and strong, and that nothing could beat me.

I had invited Chen Qingyang over to eat fish with me that night, so I was supposed to catch fish in the afternoon. But not until five o'clock did I remember I needed to go to where the fish were supposed to have been trapped to take a look. Before I reached the small fork of the rivers, two Jingpo* boys ran up,

* The Jingpo are an ethnic minority native to Yunnan, a province that borders Thailand.

hurling mud at one another all the way. Some landed on me. They stopped fighting only after I picked them up by their ears. I shouted at them, "You pricks, where're the fish?"

The older one said, "It was all that prick Le Long's fault! He sat on the dam all the time, so the dam fucking collapsed."

Le Long roared back, "Wang Er, the fucking dam you built wasn't strong enough!"

I said, "That's bullshit! I built the dam with sod. What prick has the nerve to say it wasn't strong enough?"

I went down to see for myself. Whether Le Long's fault or mine, the dam was gone anyway. The water we bailed out all flowed back, any hope of catching fish went down the drain, and the whole day went to waste. Of course, I wouldn't admit it was my fault. Instead I yelled at Le Long. Le Du (the other boy) also chimed in. Le Long began to get angry. He jumped up a couple of feet and roared, "Wang Er! Le Du! You pricks! You are ganging up on me! I'm going to tell my father. He'll shoot the two of you with his bronze-barreled shotgun!"

After saying this, the little bastard tried to leap onto the bank to escape. I caught his ankle and pulled him back. "You want to run off and leave us to herd your buffalo? You're fucking dreaming!"

The little bastard wailed *wa-wa* and tried to bite me. But I grabbed him, pinned him to the ground, and held him hard. He frothed at the mouth, cursing me in a mix of Mandarin, Jingpo, and Thai. I talked back in standard Beijing dialect. All of a sudden, he stopped cursing, eyeing the lower part of my body with envy. I looked down and found my little Buddha standing up again. I heard Le Long click his tongue admiringly, "Wow! Want to fuck Le Du's sister?"

I immediately dropped him to put on my pants.

When I lit the gas lamp at the pump house, Chen Qingyang would often arrive unexpectedly and complain that life was meaningless. She also said that she believed she was innocent in every respect. I said that the way she dared claim innocence was itself the biggest sin. In my opinion, craving good food and aversion to hard work, together with lust for beauty and sex, make up a human being's basic nature. If you were a hard worker who lived a frugal and chaste life, you would commit the sin of hypocrisy, which was more disgusting than greed, sensuality, or laziness. Words like this seemed to please her, although she never agreed with what I said out loud.

However, when I lit the gas lamp that night, she didn't show up for a long time. It was not until nine that she appeared at my door and called my name, "Wang Er, you stinker! Come out!"

I went out to see what was going on. Dressed all in white, she looked especially smart, although her expression seemed tense. She said, You invited me over to eat fish and have a heart-to-heart, but where is the fish? I had to admit that the fish were still in the river. All right, she said, at least we can still have a heart-to-heart. Then let's talk. I said, How about we go inside first? She said that's fine, too. So she went in and found herself a place to sit. She looked angry.

I had planned to seduce Chen Qingyang on my twenty-first birthday, because she was my friend; and she had a full bosom, a slender waist, and shapely buttocks; besides, her neck was long and graceful and her face was pretty, too. I wanted to have sex with her and thought she shouldn't refuse. Because if she'd needed my body to practice vivisection, I would have lent it to her without giving it a second thought; likewise, if I needed to use her body for pleasure, it shouldn't be a problem either. But she was a woman, and women in general were more or less small-minded. For that reason, I needed to expand her mind, so I began to explain what "brotherhood" was.

In my opinion, brotherhood was the kind of great friendship that only existed among the outlaws of the forest. Take the heroes in *The Legend of the Water Margins* for example. Those guys would kill and set fires as soon as eat. But as long as they heard the great name of Timely Rain,* they would fall to their knees and kowtow. Like them, I believed in nothing but brotherhood. If you were my friend, even if you committed a crime beyond Heaven's forgiveness, I would still stand by you. That night, I offered my great friendship to Chen Qingyang and she was immediately moved to tears. She accepted my friendship right away, and, what was more, even expressed her wish to reward me with a greater friendship, saying that she would never betray me even if I turned out to be a low-down, shifty

* Timely Rain is another name for the bandit Song Jiang in the novel *The Legend of the Water Margins*.

little scoundrel. Relieved by her words, naturally I told her what was really on my mind: I'm twenty-one, but I've never experienced what happens between a man and a woman. I really can't resign myself to that. She stared at me blankly after hearing my words—maybe she was not prepared for this. I kept persuading her, which didn't seem to work, so I put my hand on her shoulder and felt the tension in her muscles. The woman could change her mind any minute and slap me—if that occurred, it would only prove that women didn't understand what great friendship meant. But to my surprise, she didn't slap me. Instead she snorted and then started laughing. How stupid I am! To be tricked so easily!

What trick? What are you talking about? I played dumb.

She said, I didn't say anything. I asked her will you do it or not? She said "Pah!" and she blushed. It looked like she was a little shy, so I decided to take the initiative and began to get fresh with her. She tried to push me away a few times, and then said, No, not here. Let's go up to the mountain. So I followed her all the way up to the mountain.

Later on, Chen Qingyang told me that she had never been able to figure out whether my great friendship was true or just a lie that I had made up then to trick her. But she said that those words enchanted her like a spell, and that even if she lost everything because of it she'd have no regrets. Actually, the great friendship was neither true nor false, like everything else in the world. It was true if you believed it, and false if you didn't; my words were also neither true nor false, but I was prepared to stand by my words anytime and wouldn't back off even if the sky collapsed and the earth cracked open. Because of this attitude of mine, no one really believed me, which explained why I made no more than a couple of friends, including Chen Qingyang, even though I took it on as a lifelong cause. That night, halfway up the mountain, Chen Qingyang told me that she needed to go back to her place to get something, telling me to wait for her on the other side of the mountain. I suspected that she might want to stand me up, but I didn't say anything. I went straight to the other side of the mountain and smoked. After a while, she arrived.

Chen Qingyang said that the first time I went to her for a shot, she was dozing at her desk. In Yunnan everyone had plenty of time to nap, so they always seemed half asleep and half awake. When I walked into her clinic, the room dimmed for a moment because it was a thatched mud hut where most of the sunshine came in through the door. She awakened right then, raised her head, and asked what I was doing there. I said my lower back hurt and she told me to lie down so that she could take a look at it. I threw myself headlong onto the bamboo bed and nearly crushed it—my lower back hurt so much that I simply could not bend. If it hadn't been for that I wouldn't have gone to see her.

Chen Qingyang said my mouth had lines around it even when I was very young, and dark circles always showed under my eyes. I was a tall man of few words in worn-out clothes. She gave me a shot and I left. Maybe I thanked her, or maybe I didn't. When she had the idea I could prove she wasn't damaged goods, only half a minute passed. She ran out and found me taking a shortcut to the fourteenth team. I strode down the slope, leaping over the ditches and mounds whenever there was one, descending rapidly along the mountain slope. It was a morning in the dry season, and the wind blew up from the foot of the mountain, so I couldn't have heard anything even if she'd called me, not to mention that I never looked back anyway. So that was the way I left.

Chen Qingyang said she had wanted to go after me then, but felt it would be hard to catch up, and besides I might not be able to prove her innocence. So she walked back to the clinic. She changed her mind later because she realized since everyone accused her of being damaged goods, they were all her enemies. It was possible that I was not her enemy. She didn't want to risk turning me into an enemy also.

I smoked on the back slope of the mountain that night. Even though it was evening I could see into the distance, because the moonlight was bright, and the air was clear in that region. Every now and then, I could hear dogs barking in the distance. I spotted Chen Qingyang as soon as she came out of the fifteenth team—I doubted if I could see that far during the day. But it felt different from the day. Perhaps because there was no one around.

I couldn't tell whether there were people around or not in the evening, because it was silver-gray everywhere. If you traveled with a torch, it meant you wanted the whole world to know where you were; if you didn't, it would be like wearing a cape of invisibility—people who knew you were there could see you, and people who didn't couldn't. When I saw Chen Qingyang slowly coming toward me, my heart began to pound, and it occurred to me without any instruction that we should have a little foreplay before getting down to business.

Chen Qingyang reacted pretty coldly to this. Her lips were icy, and she didn't respond to my caresses at all. By the time I tried to unbutton her dress, all thumbs, she pushed me away and started taking off her clothes by herself, piece by piece. She folded her clothes neatly and put them aside. Then she lay down stiffly on the grass.

Her naked body was extremely beautiful. I took off my clothes in a hurry and crawled over to her. Again she pushed me off, handing me something, saying, "Know how to use this? Want me to teach you?"

It was a condom. I was at the height of my excitement and the tone of her voice upset me a little. But I put on the condom anyway and crawled on top of her. Heart racing and out of breath, I fumbled for quite a while and couldn't get it right. Again I heard her cold voice, "Hey, do you know what you're doing?"

I said, Of course I do. Could you please move a little closer? I want to study your anatomy in the light. Then with a sound as loud as a thunderclap at my ear, I realized she'd given me a big slap. I jumped to my feet, grabbed my clothes, and ran.

3

I did not leave that night—Chen Qingyang caught me and asked me to stay in the name of our great friendship. She admitted that she'd been wrong to slap me, and that she hadn't treated me well. But she said my great friendship was phony, and the reason I had tricked her into coming was to study her anatomy. I said if she thought I was a faker, why did she believe me? I did want to study her anatomy, but that was with her permission, too. If she didn't like the idea, she could have told me before. In any case, slapping me was unfair. She laughed hard for a while and said she simply couldn't bear the sight of that thing on my body. It looked silly and shameless, and whenever she saw him, she just couldn't help getting angry.

We didn't have a stitch on while we argued. My little Buddha still stuck out, glittering in the moonlight as if wrapped in plastic. I was a little offended by what she said and she realized that too. So to make peace, she softened her tone and said, "Anyway, he is breathtakingly ugly—don't you agree?"

Standing there like an angry cobra, the thing was indeed homely. I said, since you don't even want to look at him, let's just forget the whole thing. I began to put on my pants, but again she said, Don't! So I started smoking. The moment I had the cigarette finished, she embraced me and we did it on the grass.

Until my twenty-first birthday I was a virgin, but that night I lured Chen Qingyang up the mountain with me. At first there was moonlight, then the moon set and a sky full of stars came out, as numerous as dewdrops in the morning. There was no wind that night either; the mountain was very still. Having made love to Chen Qingyang, I was no longer a virgin. However, I wasn't feeling happy at all. That was because when I was doing it, she didn't make a sound; she simply put her arms under her head and looked at me in a very thoughtful way. So from beginning to end it was just my solo performance. In fact, I didn't last too long. I finished almost right away. After that I was angry and upset.

Chen Qingyang said she couldn't believe it: I actually had the impudence to display my ugly male organ in front of her, without feeling the least embarrassed. The thing didn't feel embarrassed either; it just forced its way straight into the hole between her thighs. Because there is this hole in a woman's body, a man thinks he has to use it, which just doesn't make sense. When she had a husband before, he did this to her every day. All the time she kept the question to herself, waiting for the day when he felt ashamed of himself and would explain why he did this to her. But he never apologized, and then he went to prison. These were things I didn't want to hear. So I asked her if she hadn't felt like doing it, why had she agreed? She said she didn't want to be considered small-minded. I said, You're a small-minded person anyway. Then she said, Never mind, let's not fight about it. She told me to return that evening, and we'd try it one more time. Maybe she'd like it. I didn't say anything. In the foggy dawn, I left her and went down the mountain to herd buffalo.

I didn't go to see her that night, instead I went to the hospital, the reason being: when I got to the cattle pen in the morning, a bunch of people couldn't wait for me and had opened the pen and dragged the buffalo out. Everyone was trying to pick out a strong one for plowing the fields. A local youth called Shan Men Er was pulling out a large white one. I went over to tell him that the buffalo had been bitten by a poisonous snake and couldn't work. He didn't seem to hear me, so I snatched the tether from him and he slapped me without thinking. I shoved him right in the chest, pushing him down on his butt. Then people began to gather, forming a tight ring around us and urging us to fight. With the students from Beijing on one side and the country boys on the other, everyone chose a weapon, either a wooden stick or a leather belt. They argued for a while, then decided not to fight but to make Shan Men Er and I wrestle. Unable to beat me at wrestling, Shan Men Er began to punch me. I kicked him into a manure pit right in front of the cattle pen for a shit bath. He got up, grabbed a pitchfork, and tried to stab me, but somebody stopped him.

That was what happened in the morning. When I came back from herding buffalo in the evening, the team leader accused me of beating peasants, saying that he was going to call a meeting to denounce me. I told him that he could take his chances and give me trouble, but I was no pushover. I also told him that I would get some people together for a gang fight. The team leader said he didn't want to give me a hard time; it was Shan Men Er's mother who was giving him a hard time. The woman was a widow, a real bitch. He said that's the way it goes around here. Later he said he was not going to arrange a denouncing meeting but a helping meeting. I could just stand in front of people and do a self-criticism. If I still didn't agree, he was going to let the widow come after me.

The meeting was a complete mess. The locals all talked at once, saying that the city students had gone too far—we not only took their chickens and stole their dogs, but also beat their people. The city students said, That's bullshit! Who stole your chickens and dogs? Did you catch us in the act? We're here to build up our country's borderland. We aren't some criminals in exile. Why should we put up with casual slander? Standing in front of the crowd, I didn't do self-criticism but called them names. I didn't expect Shan Men Er's mother to sneak up from behind, pick up a heavy stool, and slam my lower back, right on my old injury. I passed out instantly.

By the time I came around, Luo Xiaosi had gathered a group of city students and was threatening to burn the cattle pen. He also said he'd make Shan Men Er's mother pay with her life. The team leader took a bunch of locals to stop them. Meanwhile, the vice team leader told someone to take me to the hospital on an ox cart. The nurse said they shouldn't try to move me since my back was broken, and I'd be done for. I said, My back seems OK and you guys can just carry me. However, since none of them was sure about whether or not my back was broken, they were all afraid to move me. So I had no choice but to stay put. Finally, the team leader came over and said, Go phone Chen Qingyang. Let her check his back. After a short while, Chen Qingyang ran over, with messy hair and puffy eyelids. The first thing she said was: Don't worry. If you're paralyzed, I'll take care of you for the rest of my life. Then she checked my back and her diagnosis was the same as mine. So they carried me to the ox cart and sent me to the hospital at the farm headquarters.

That night Chen Qingyang accompanied me to the hospital and waited until the x-ray of my lower back was developed. She left after making sure everything was fine. She said she would come back to visit me in a couple of days, but she never did. I was hospitalized for a whole week, and once I could get around, I went straight back to see her.

When I walked into Chen Qingyang's clinic, I carried so many things on my back that my pack was overflowing. In addition to a wok, bowls, a basin, and ladle, there was enough food for two of us to eat for an entire month. When she saw me come into her clinic, she gave me a faint smile and said, Are you completely recovered? Where are you going with all that stuff?

I said I was going to the Qingping thermal springs to bathe. She leaned back languidly in her chair and said, That's a great idea. The thermal springs might cure your old injury. I said I wasn't really going to the thermal springs. I just wanted to stay on the back slope of the mountain for a few days. She said there is nothing on the back of the mountain. Better go to the thermal springs.

The Qingping thermal springs were mud pools located in a valley, surrounded by nothing but wild, grassy hills. The people who built huts on the hills and lived there year-round were usually patients with a variety of diseases. If I went there, not only wouldn't it cure the pain in my lower back, but worse, I might get leprosy. However, the lowland on the back slope of the deserted mountain was crisscrossed with gullies and ditches; and fragrant grass grew lush in the sparse woods. I could build a thatched hut in some deserted spot, an empty mountain with no human trace—gurgling water with fallen petals. A place like that would help cultivate morality and nourish the inner nature. When Chen Qingyang heard this she couldn't help smiling. How do you get to that place? Maybe I'll go there to visit you. I gave her directions and even made a map for her, and then went into the mountains alone.

After I got to the desolate mountainside, Chen Qingyang didn't come to see me right away. The strong wind of the dry season blew endlessly, shaking the thatched hut. Sitting in a chair and listening to the sound of the wind, Chen Qingyang would look back at what happened and begin to have doubts about everything. It was hard for her to believe that she had come to these backwoods in a haze, had begun to be called damaged goods for no reason, and then turned into real damaged goods. The whole thing was just unbelievable.

Chen Qingyang said that sometimes she would step out of her room and look in the direction of the back slope of the mountain, seeing the many paths winding through the valley and leading deep into the mountains. My words still echoed in her ears. She knew that any of those paths would take her to me. There was no doubt about it. But the more certain something was, the more doubtful it became. Maybe the path didn't lead anywhere; maybe Wang Er was not in the mountains; maybe Wang Er didn't exist at all.

A couple of days later, Luo Xiaosi brought several people to the hospital to see me. No one in the hospital had ever heard of Wang Er, so nobody knew where he had gone. At the time the hospital was rampant with hepatitis. The uninfected patients all fled to their homes to recuperate, and the doctors went down to the production team to provide medical care. Luo Xiaosi came back to the fourteenth team and found my stuff gone, so he went to ask the team leader whether he had seen me. The team leader said, Who's Wang Er? Never heard of him. Luo Xiaosi said, Just a few days ago you called a meeting to denounce him, and the vixen hit him with a stool and almost killed him. Having been reminded that way, the team leader was even more reluctant to refresh his memory about me. It just so happened that at the time a relief delegation from Beijing was coming to investigate how the city students were treated in the countryside, especially whether any had been tied up, beaten, or forced to marry the locals. Because of this, the team leader was even more unwilling to remember me. Luo Xiaosi then made his way to the fifteenth team, asking Chen Qingyang whether she had seen me, and hinting in a roundabout sort of way that she'd had an indecent relationship with me. Chen Qingyang then told him that she knew nothing about me.

By the time Luo Xiaosi left, Chen Qingyang was confused. It seemed many people didn't believe Wang Er so much as existed. That's what confused people. What everyone thinks exists must not exist, because everything before our eyes is illusion; what everyone doesn't think exists must exist, like Wang Er. If he didn't exist, where did his name come from? Unable to overcome her curiosity, Chen Qingyang finally dropped everything and went up the mountain to look for me.

After the vixen knocked me out with a stool, Chen Qingyang ran all the way down the mountain to see me. She even cried in public and declared that if I didn't recover, she would take care of me all her life. It turned out not only did I live, but I wasn't even paralyzed, which was a good thing for me though she wasn't crazy about it. It was almost as if she'd confessed publicly that she was damaged goods. If I'd died, or become paralyzed, it would have then been morally justified. But I had only stayed in the hospital for a week and then run away. To her, I was the precise image of someone seen from behind, hurrying down the mountain, a man in her memory. She didn't want to make love to me, nor did she want to carry on a love affair with me either. So, without a very important reason, her visiting me would be the act of a woman who was truly damaged goods.

Chen Qingyang said that when she decided to head up the mountain to search for me, she didn't have anything on under her white smock. Dressed like this, she crossed a stretch of hills behind the fifteenth team. Those hills were thick with grass, and under the grass lay red soil. In the morning the wind blew down the mountain to the plateau, cold as a mountain spring, and in the afternoon the wind returned, full of heat and dust. Chen

Qingyang came riding on a white wind to look for me. The wind got under her clothes and flowed all over her body, like caresses and lips. In fact, she didn't really need me, nor did she have to find me. When people said she was damaged goods and I was her lover, she came to see me every day. It seemed necessary back then, though. Ever since she admitted in public she was damaged goods, and I was her lover, no one said she was damaged goods anymore, let alone mentioned my name in front of her (except for Luo Xiaosi). People were so afraid of this kind of damaged-goods behavior in broad daylight that they didn't even dare talk about it.

As for the Beijing relief delegation sent to investigate the city students' situation, everyone in the local area knew about it except for me. That was because lately I had been off herding buffalo, which required going out early in the morning and coming back late at night; besides that, I had a bad reputation and no one bothered to tell me. Later, when I was in the hospital, nobody came to see me either. When I left the hospital, I went deep into the mountains almost right away. I saw only two people before my trip, one of whom was Chen Qingyang, who hadn't mentioned it; the other one was our team leader, who also hadn't said anything other than telling me to take a good rest at the thermal springs. I told him that I didn't have anything (food, utensils, etc.), so I couldn't go to the thermal springs. He said he could lend me some things. I told him that I might not be able to return them. He said it didn't matter. So I borrowed plenty of homemade smoked meat and sausages.

Chen Qingyang didn't give me the information because she didn't care about it—she was not one of the city students. The team leader didn't tell me because he thought I knew already. He also thought that since I took so much food with me I probably wouldn't come back. That was why when Luo Xiaosi asked him where Wang Er had gone, he said, Wang Er? Who's Wang Er? Never heard of him. For those like Luo Xiaosi, it would have been a great advantage to find me—I could prove that the city students in the area were treated badly, often beaten senseless. For our team leader, my nonexistence was very convenient, because then no one could prove any of the city students had been beaten senseless. To me, it didn't really matter whether I existed or not. If no one came to look for me, I could grow some corn around the place and never leave. So I didn't really care whether I existed or not.

I also thought about the problem of whether I existed or not in my little thatched hut. For example, others believed that Chen Qingyang had slept with me and that proved my existence. In Luo Xiaosi's words, Wang Er and Chen Qingyang took off their pants and screwed. Actually he didn't see any of it, but the extent of his imagination was that we took off our pants. And there was Chen Qingyang, who said that I hurried down the mountain in my green fatigues. It never crossed my mind that I didn't look back as I walked. Since I couldn't imagine these things, they must be evidence of my existence.

Then there was this little Buddha of mine, stiff and straight, and that was something I couldn't invent either. I always expected Chen Qingyang to come to see me, but she never came. By the time she finally showed up, I had learned not to expect her.

4

I used to believe that Chen Qingyang would come to see me immediately after I went up the mountain, but I was wrong. I waited for a long time and then decided to give up. I sat in my little hut, listening to the leaves rustling all over the mountain, finally reaching a state where object and subject were both forgotten. I listened to the mighty air currents surging over my head, and just then a wave rose from my soul, as flowers bloom in the midst of the mountains and bamboo husks fall from the shoots and the bamboo stands up straight. When the wave receded, I would rest calmly, but I wanted to dance while the wave was at its peak. Chen Qingyang arrived at my thatched hut precisely at that moment and caught sight of me sitting naked on the bamboo bed. My penis was like a skinned rabbit, red, shiny, and a foot long, frankly erect. Panicked, Chen Qingyang immediately screamed.

Chen Qingyang's search for me could be summed up as follows: Two weeks after I went into the mountains, she went up the mountains to look for me. It was only two o'clock in the afternoon, but she took off her underwear, like women who sneak out for sex at midnight, and wore only a white smock, walking barefoot in the mountains. She crossed a sunlit meadow, entered a dry gully, and walked for a long time. Even through the maze of gullies, she didn't make a single wrong turn. Later she emerged from the gully, walked into a valley facing the sun, and saw a thatched hut that seemed newly built. If there had been no Wang Er to tell her the route, she wouldn't have been able to find such a tiny hut in the vast, wild mountains. But as she entered the hut and saw Wang Er sitting on the bed, his little Buddha stiff, she was frightened into screaming.

Later Chen Qingyang said she just couldn't believe everything she had experienced was real, because something real needs to have a cause. Yet at the time she just took off her white smock, sat beside me, and stared at my little Buddha, thinking he was the color of a burn scar. Just then my thatched hut began to shake in the wind, streams of sunlight leaked through the roof and spattered her body, like stars. I reached out my hand and touched her nipples, until her face flushed and her nipples turned hard. Suddenly she woke from her trance, her face blushing with embarrassment. Then she embraced me tightly.

It was the second time that I made love to Chen Qingyang. When we first made love, many details puzzled me. Not until much later did I finally figure out how much she had really taken to heart being called damaged goods. Since she couldn't prove she wasn't damaged goods, she consented to becoming damaged goods, like the women caught in the act and summoned on stage to confess the details of their adultery. The confessions would reach a point when the audience, unable to restrain themselves, their faces twisted into hundreds of masks of lust, would shout, Tie her up! Then someone would rush onto the stage and bind her into the loops of a five-petal knot with thin hemp twine. She stood like this in front of the crowd, submitting herself to all the shame and insults. That didn't bother her at all. She wouldn't have been afraid of being stripped naked, strapped to a millstone, and thrown into a pond; nor would she have feared being forced to dress up, like the wives and concubines of wealthy men, their faces covered with water-soaked yellow paper, sitting upright until they smothered to death. No, these things wouldn't have bothered her at all. She was not the least bit worried about becoming actual damaged goods, which she much preferred to being damaged goods in name only. What disgusted her was the act that made her damaged goods.

When I made love to Chen Qingyang, a lizard crawled out of a crack in the wall and crossed the ground in the middle of the room, moving intermittently. Then suddenly startled, it fled quickly, disappearing into the sunshine outside the door. Just at that moment Chen Qingyang's moans flooded out, filling the entire room. I was scared and stopped, leaning over her body. But she pinched my leg and said: Hurry, you idiot! I sped up and waves of vibration passed through me as if from the earth's core. Afterward, she said she had fallen deep into sin and karma would catch up with her sooner or later.

When she said that, the band of flush was fading from her chest. At the time we hadn't finished our business yet. So she made it sound like she would only be punished for what she had just done. Suddenly a shudder traveled from the top of my head to my tailbone and I began to ejaculate wildly. Since this had nothing to do with her, perhaps I would be the only one punished for it.

Later Chen Qingyang told me that Luo Xiaosi had looked for me everywhere. He went to the hospital, and people there told him that I didn't exist; then he went to our team leader, who also said that I didn't exist; finally, he went to Chen Qingyang. Chen Qingyang told him that since everyone said he didn't exist, maybe he didn't. She had no problem with that. When he heard this, Luo Xiaosi couldn't help crying.

I felt very strange after I heard her words. I shouldn't come into existence simply because a vixen hit me, nor should I stop existing because she hit me. Actually, my existence was an indisputable fact. So I became obsessed. To prove the indisputable fact, I went down the mountain the day the relief delegation arrived and took part in the delegation's hearing. After the hearing, the team leader said, You don't look sick at all. I think you'd better come back to feed the pigs. He also arranged for people to trail Chen Qingyang and me, trying to catch us in the act of adultery. Of course, it was not easy to catch me because I walked so fast. No one could successfully track me. However, this got me into a lot more trouble. By then I began to realize that it was really unnecessary for me to prove my existence to others.

When I fed the pigs for the production team, every day I had to carry buckets of water. It was really a tiring job, and impossible to slack off. The pigs would squeal if they didn't get enough food. I had to chop tons of vegetables and cut piles of wood. Originally there had been three women to do the job, but now the team leader assigned it all to me. I found that I could not manage three women's work, especially when my back hurt. I really wanted to prove that I didn't exist then.

At night Chen Qingyang and I would make love in my small hut. In those days, I was full of respect for the task, enthusiastic about every kiss and caress. Whether it was the classical missionary position, or man-from-behind position, man-from-side position, or woman-on-top position, I performed them in sober earnest. Chen Qingyang was very satisfied with my performance, and so was I. At those moments, I felt it was unnecessary to prove my existence. I drew a conclusion from these experiences: never let other people pay attention to you! Beijingers say: Better a thief should steal from you than keep you in mind. You should never let other people keep you in mind.

After a while, the city students in our team were all transferred to other positions; the men landed work at the candy factory, and the women got to teach at the agricultural middle school. I was the only one left feeding those pigs. According to them that was because I was not reeducated enough, but Chen Qingyang said it was because someone kept me in mind. This "someone" might have been the military deputy on our farm. She also said the military deputy was a jerk. She used to work in the hospital, but when the military deputy tried to grope her, she gave him a big slap, and afterward, she was sent down to the fifteenth production team to work as a team doctor. The fifteenth team's water was bitter, and there wasn't much to eat either. She got used to it after a while. But it was clear from the start the military deputy just wanted to make trouble for her. Chen Qingyang said that the military deputy would definitely not go easy on me, perhaps I would be kept-in-mind half to death. I said: What can he do to me? If things get really bad, I can simply run the hell away. What happened later all started there.

That morning, right at dawn, I went down the mountain to feed the pigs. As I passed the village well, I saw the military deputy at the well stand brushing his teeth. He took the brush out of his mouth and talked to me with a mouth full of froth. I thought he was very disgusting, so I left without a word. Shortly afterward, he ran to the pigpen and shouted at me: How dare you walk away from me like that? I kept silent as I heard the words. Even when he accused me of playing dumb, I still said nothing. After a while I walked away again.

The military deputy came to our team to do some grassroots investigation and then stayed. According to him, he wouldn't give up until he made Wang Er talk. His visit could be accounted for in two ways: one was that he came down to our team for the investigation, but when he met someone like me who played dumb with him, he got pissed off and decided to stay; the other was that he came down to our team not for investigation, but to pick on me, after hearing that Chen Qingyang and I had a love affair. Whatever brought him to our team, I made up my mind to stay mute. He couldn't do anything about it.

The military deputy had a talk with me, asking me to write a confession. He said that the masses were very angry about my love affair with Chen Qingyang. If I didn't confess, he would mobilize the masses to deal with me. He also said my behavior met the criteria for my classification as one of "the bad elements," and I should be punished by the proletarian dictatorship. I could have defended myself by saying I didn't have a love affair. Who could prove I did? But I just stared at him, like a wild boar, like an idiot, like a male cat staring at a female one, until his anger vanished under my stare. Then he let me go.

In the end, he still couldn't get anything out of me. He wasn't even sure whether I was a mute or not. People told him that I wasn't a mute. He couldn't be sure since he had never heard me speak a single word. To this day, whenever he thinks of me, he still can't figure out if I am mute or not. It makes me very happy whenever I think about it.

5

Finally we were taken into custody and forced to write confessions for a long time. At first I wrote the following: Chen Qingyang and I have an indecent relationship. That was all. But it came down from above that what I wrote was too simple, and they asked me to start over. Later on I wrote that Chen Qingyang and I had an indecent relationship, and that I had screwed her many times, and she liked being screwed by me. This time the opinions from above said it needed more detail. So I added detail: The fortieth time that we made illegal love, the location was the thatched hut I secretly built on the mountain. It was either the fifteenth or the sixteenth by the lunar calendar—whatever the date, the moon shone brightly. Chen Qingyang sat on the bamboo bed, her body gleaming in the moonlight that shone through the door. I stood on the ground, and she locked her legs around my waist. We chatted for a while. I told her that her breasts were not just full, but also shapely; her navel not only round, but shallow too. All of this was very good. She said, Really? I had no idea. After a while the moonlight moved away. I lit a cigarette, but she took it from me after I finished half of it, taking several drags. She pinched my nose, for the locals believed that a virgin's nose would be very hard, and a man dying of too much sex would have a soft nose. On some of these occasions she lazed on the bed, leaning against the bamboo wall; other times she held me like a koala bear, blowing warm breath on my face. At last the moonlight shone through the window opposite the door and we were separate by then. However, I wrote these confessions not for the military deputy—he was no longer our military deputy, having been discharged from the army and gone back home. It didn't matter whether he was our military deputy or not, we had to write confessions about our errors anyway.

Years later, I had a good relationship with the director of personnel at our school. He told me that the great thing about the job was that you could read other people's confessions, which I believe included mine. I thought of all the confessions mine would be the richest and most vivid. That was because I wrote it in a hotel, with nothing else to do, like a professional writer.

In the evening I made my escape. That morning, I asked the mess officer for a day off because I needed to go to Jingkan to buy toothpaste. I worked under the mess officer, who also had the task of watching me. He was supposed to keep an eye on me every minute, but I disappeared as soon as it got dark. In the morning I brought him a lot of loquats, all very good. The loquats growing on the plain aren't edible, because of the ant colonies in them. Only the ones on the mountain don't have ants. The mess officer said since we got along, and the military deputy wasn't around, he'd allow me to go buy toothpaste. But he also said the military deputy might return any minute. If I were not here by the time the military deputy returned, he couldn't cover for me. I left my team and climbed to the fifteenth team's mountainside, holding a small piece of mirror to reflect light on Chen Qingyang's back window. After a while, she came up the mountain and told me that since people had been keeping a close eye on her for the past two days, she hadn't been able to get out. And right now she was having her period. She said that shouldn't be a problem and we could still do it. I said that wasn't going to work. When we said goodbye to each other, she insisted on giving me two hundred yuan. I refused at first, but then took it after a while.

Later Chen Qingyang told me that nobody had been keeping a close eye on her those two days, and she hadn't been having her period when she saw me. In fact, people in the fifteenth team didn't pay attention to her at all. People there were used to accusing the innocent of being damaged goods, but as for real damaged goods, they just let them do whatever they wanted. The reason that she didn't come up the mountain and kept me waiting for nothing was because she began to feel tired of it. She couldn't do it unless she was in the right mood; having sex wouldn't necessarily put her in a good mood. Of course, after her deception she felt guilty. That was why she gave me two hundred yuan. I thought since she might have trouble spending the two hundred yuan, I wouldn't mind helping her. So I brought the money with me to Jingkan and bought a double-barreled shotgun for myself.

Later when I wrote my confessions, the double-barreled shotgun was also an issue. They suspected that I might want to kill someone with it. Actually, if I'd wanted to kill someone, it wouldn't have made any difference whether I used a two hundred-yuan double-barreled shotgun or a forty-yuan bronze-barreled gun. A bronze-barreled gun, normally used to shoot wild ducks by the water, was not practical at all in the mountains; besides, it was as heavy as a corpse. When I got to the street in Jingkan that day, it was already afternoon, and since it wasn't a market day, there was just a deserted dirt road and a few deserted state-run stores. Inside one store a saleswoman dozed while a swarm of flies circled around. The shelf display read "aloomenum wokk" and "aloomenum kittel," and underneath were aluminum woks and aluminum kettles. I chatted awhile with the saleswoman, who was from Shandong Province, and she let me go in their storeroom to look around myself. In there I saw a shotgun made in Shanghai. So I bought it even though it had sat there for nearly two years. At dusk I tested it on the riverbank and killed a heron. The military deputy happened to return from the farm headquarters right then and was shocked to see my shotgun. He went on about how it was not right that everyone could have a gun, and that someone had to talk to the team leader and confiscate Wang Er's gun. When I heard this, I felt the urge to fire at his belly. If I had, it would probably have killed him. Then most likely I wouldn't be around today.

On the way back from Jingkan that afternoon, I waded through the paddy field and stood among the rice seedlings for a while. I saw leeches swimming out like fish and sticking to my legs. I was naked to the waist then, because I had used my clothes to wrap brown sugar buns (the only kind of food sold in the town's restaurant), and with the buns in my hands and a gun slung over my back, I felt really loaded down. So I ignored the leeches. Only when I got up the bank did I start pulling them off one by one and burning them. They turned soft and blistery in the fire. All of a sudden, I felt very frustrated and tired, nothing like a twenty-one-year-old. I realized I would get old quickly if things continued like this.

After a while, I ran into Le Du, who told me that they had caught all the fish at the fork of the rivers. My share had been dried into stockfish and stored at his sister's place. His sister wanted me to come get it. I knew his sister very well; she was a dark, pretty girl. I told him that I couldn't get there for a while. I gave him all my brown sugar buns and asked him to take a message to the fifteenth team, telling Chen Qingyang that I'd bought a gun with her money. Le Du went to the fifteenth team and told Chen Qingyang. She was afraid that I might shoot the military deputy. This concern was not completely unreasonable. By the evening I really began to consider taking a shot at the military deputy.

At dusk, when I shot the heron by the river, I ran into the military deputy. As usual, I stayed mute and he kept nagging at me. I got really angry. For more than two weeks, he had been holding forth on the same subject over and over, that I was a bad person and needed thought reform. People shouldn't let up on me for a minute. I'd been hearing that sort of thing all my life but never got angrier than that night. After a while, he said he had wonderful good news to announce later that day, but wouldn't reveal what it was except that "the rotten whore" Chen Qingyang and I were going to have a really hard time from now on. Infuriated by what he said, I was tempted to choke him right on the spot, but my curiosity about the great news got the better of me. However, he went on talking nonsense to keep me guessing. Not until we reached our team did he say, Come to the meeting tonight. I'll announce the news at the meeting.

But I didn't go to the meeting that evening. I packed my stuff, ready to flee back to the mountains. I believed that some major event must have happened to give the military deputy a way to take care of Chen Qingyang and me. As for what the event was, I couldn't figure it out—in those days anything could happen. I even imagined that the emperor had been restored and the military deputy had become the local chief. He could castrate me with a hammer and then take Chen Qingyang as his concubine. By the time I finished my packing and was about to leave, I realized that things were not that bad. People were shouting slogans at the meeting that I could hear even from my room. It turned out that our state-run farm had been changed into an Army Production Corps, and the military deputy might be promoted to Regimental Commander. At any rate, he couldn't castrate me, or take Chen Qingyang as his concubine. After a few minutes' hesitation, I slung the pack on my back. Then I hacked up everything in the place with a machete, found a piece of charcoal, and wrote "x x x (the military deputy's name), fuck your mother!" on the wall. After that I left and headed up the mountain.

That was how I ran away from the fourteenth team. I also included these things in my confessions. To summarize, it went like this: The military deputy had a personal grudge against me, which was twofold. Firstly, I told the relief delegation that I had been beaten unconscious, which made the military deputy lose face; secondly, he and I fought over a woman, which was why he was always trying to screw me. So, when I learned he was about to become Regimental Commander, I felt that I couldn't take it anymore and fled into the mountains. Even today I still believe that was the true reason for my escape. But they said that the military deputy hadn't become Regimental Commander, so my explanation for running away wouldn't stand up. So, they said my confessions were unconvincing. A convincing confession would be that Chen Qingyang and I were having a love affair. As the saying goes: For sex, a man would dare anything. We would do anything for it—well, there's some truth to that. But when I ran away from our team, I didn't plan to see Chen Qingyang, thinking that I could just leave without telling anyone. When I reached the edge of the mountains I realized that after all Chen Qingyang was a friend of mine and I should go back to say goodbye to her. I hadn't expected Chen Qingyang to say she wanted to run away with me. She said if she didn't join me in such an adventure, we would throw our great friendship to the dogs. So she packed some stuff in a hurry and took off with me. Without her and what she packed, I would have gotten sick and died on the mountain for sure. The supplies she packed included lots of malaria medicine, and plenty of jumbo-sized condoms.

After Chen Qingyang and I escaped to the mountains, the farm panicked for a while. They believed we had run off to Burma. It wouldn't have been good for any of us if that news had gotten out. So they didn't report us, only issued a wanted poster on the farm. Both Chen Qingyang and I were easily recognized, and, besides, the double-barreled shotgun we brought along was hard to hide. But for some reason nobody found us until half a year later when each of us returned to our own teams. And then after another month, the public security section summoned us to write our confessions. It was our bad luck to be the victims of a new political campaign and have someone inform on us.

6

The office of public security was located at the entrance to our farm's headquarters. It was a lonely mud-brick house. You could see it from far off, because it was whitewashed and set on a hill. When people went to the market at headquarters, they could see it from a distance. A patch of sisal hemp, a perennial dark green in color, surrounded the house, but the clay underneath was red. I confessed my errors there, making a clean breast of everything. We went up the mountains, and first we planted some corn on the back slope of the fifteenth team. The soil there was poor, and half the corn didn't grow. And then we left, sleeping in the daytime and walking at night, looking for other places to settle. Finally we remembered an abandoned mill on the mountain, where there was a large, deserted area of fertile ground. Since an escapee from the leper colony, whom people called Grandpa Liu, lived there, no one visited except Chen Qingyang, prompted by her sense of duty as a doctor. We finally went there for shelter, living in the valley behind the mill. Chen Qingyang treated Grandpa Liu's leprosy, and I tended the land for him. After a while, I traveled to the market in Qingping and ran into some classmates. They told me that the military deputy had been transferred someplace else and nobody remembered our affair anymore. So we came back. That was how the whole business went.

I remained in the public security section for a long time. For a while the atmosphere was not bad. They said my problem was pretty clear and all I needed to do was to write confessions. But after a while the situation turned more serious; they suspected that we had gone abroad, colluded with the enemy, and come back on a mission. So they took Chen Qingyang to the office, interrogating her severely. While they interrogated her, I looked out the window—the sky was filled with clouds.

They wanted me to confess how I had slipped across the border. As far as border-crossing went, I wasn't completely innocent. I did cross the border. I disguised myself as a Thai to go to the market on the other side. I bought a few boxes of matches and salt. But it was unnecessary to tell them about this. Things unnecessary to say shouldn't be said.

Later I led those security people to our place to investigate. The thatched hut that I built on the back slope of the fifteenth team had leaks in the roof, the cornfield attracted many birds, and the heap of used condoms behind our hut supplied ironclad evidence of our former occupancy. The locals didn't like to use condoms, holding that condoms block exchange between yin and yang and gradually weaken people. Actually, those local condoms were better than any other ones I used later. They were made of 100 percent natural rubber.

Afterward I refused to take them there again. Anyway, I told them I had never crossed the border, and they didn't believe me; I showed them the place, but they still didn't believe me. Things unnecessary to do shouldn't be done. I stayed mute all day long, and so did Chen Qingyang. The investigators asked us questions at first, but got lazy after a while. On market day, many Thais and Jingpos came by, carrying fresh fruits and vegetables on their backs, and our interrogators got fewer and fewer. Finally there was only one person left. He also wanted to go to the market, but it wasn't time to release us yet and leaving us unattended was against the rules. So he went outside to call someone. He ordered a few passing women to stop. They didn't stop but sped up. We smiled when we saw this.

The security comrade finally stopped a woman. Chen Qingyang rose to her feet, smoothed out her hair, straightened the collar of her shirt, and then turned around, putting her hands behind her back. The woman tied her up, starting from her hands and then running the rope over her neck and arms to make a knot. She apologized, I'm just hopeless at tying people up. The security comrade said, That's good enough. Then he tied me up, sat us back-to-back in two separate chairs, and roped the whole thing together. He locked the door and went to the market. After a long time, he came back to get something from the office desk. He asked, Want to go to the bathroom? It's still early. I'll come back after a while and then let you two leave. Then he went out again.

When he finally came to set us free, Chen Qingyang wiggled her fingers, smoothed her hair, and brushed the dust from her clothes. Then we returned to our hotel room. We went to the public security section every day and would be tied up every market day. Beyond that, we had to go to every team to accept public denouncement with other bad elements. They threatened, more than once, to use other methods of the proletarian dictatorship on us—that was how our investigation went.

Later on they stopped suspecting we had gone abroad. They began to deal with Chen Qingyang in a more civilized way, often asking her to go to the hospital and treat the prostatitis of the chief of staff. At that time, our farm had admitted a large number of retired army cadres, many of whom suffered from prostatitis. Through the investigation, they found that Chen Qingyang was the only one on our entire farm who knew there was such a thing as a prostate gland in a human. The security comrades told us to confess our love affair. I said, How do you know we had a love affair? Did you see it? They said, Then confess your speculation problem. Again I asked, How do you know I had a speculation problem? They said, A traitorship problem would do. Anyway, you have to confess something. As far as what specific problem you want to confess, that's up to you. If you confess nothing, we won't release you. After discussing it, Chen Qingyang and I decided to confess our love affair. She said, Things we actually did we shouldn't be afraid to confess.

That was how I got started writing confessions like a writer. The first thing I confessed was what happened the night we ran away. After a few drafts, I finally wrote that Chen Qingyang looked like a koala bear. She admitted that she was very excited that night and really felt like a koala bear. She finally had a chance to fulfill her great friendship. So she locked her legs around my waist, grabbed my shoulder with her hands, and imagining that I was a tall tree, tried to climb up several times.

When I saw Chen Qingyang again, it was already the nineties. She told me that she had divorced her husband and was now living with her daughter in Shanghai. She came to Beijing on a business trip. As soon as she got to Beijing, she began to recall that Wang Er lived here and she might be able to see me. Subsequently, she did run into me at Dragon-Lair Lake Temple Fair. I had the same old look—deep wrinkles stretching toward my mouth, dark circles under my eyes, and I wore an old-fashioned cotton jacket. Squatting on the ground, I was eating spiced giblets and baked pancakes that fancy places wouldn't serve. The only difference was that my fingers had been burned yellow by nitric acid.

Chen Qingyang had changed a lot. She wore a thin beige coat, a tweed skirt, high-heeled leather boots and a pair of gold-rimmed glasses, like a public relations person in a big company. If she hadn't called my name, I wouldn't have recognized her. At that moment it dawned on me that everyone had his own essence, which would shine in the right setting. I was essentially a rascal or bandit. Now that I was a city dweller and a schoolteacher, mine didn't look quite right.

Chen Qingyang said her daughter had gone into her sophomore year at the university. Recently she found out about our affair and wanted to meet me. What occasioned this was: Her hospital wanted to promote Chen Qingyang, but they found this pile of confessions in her dossier. After a discussion, the leaders decided they were persecutory materials from the Cultural Revolution and should be discarded. So they sent someone to Yunnan to investigate her case, spent over ten thousand yuan on the trip, and finally removed all the confessions from the file. Since she was the author, they returned them to her. She brought them home and stashed them somewhere, and her daughter found them. Her daughter said, Wow! So that's how the two of you made me.

Actually, I had nothing to do with her daughter. When her daughter was conceived, I had already left Yunnan. Chen Qingyang explained things to her daughter that way, too. But the girl said I could have put my sperm in a test tube and mailed it to Chen Qingyang, who was still in Yunnan at that time, for artificial insemination. In her words, "There's nothing you pair of jerks wouldn't do."

The first night we escaped to the mountains, Chen Qingyang was very aroused. When I finally got to sleep at daybreak, she woke me again. At that time fog was pouring through the crack in the wall. She wanted me to do it again, telling me not to wear the rubber thing. She was going to have a brood of babies with me. Let them hang down to here in a few years. Meanwhile, she pulled her breasts down by the nipples to show me where they would reach. But I didn't like the idea that her breasts would droop and said, Let's think of a way to keep them from drooping. That was why I continued to wear the rubber thing. After that she lost interest in making love to me.

When I saw Chen Qingyang all those years later, I asked, How are they? Did they droop? She said, You bet they did. They're as droopy as hell. Want to see the droop? I got to see them shortly after—they weren't that bad. But she said, They will be that bad sooner or later. There's no way out.

When I turned in this confession, the leaders really liked it. One big shot, either the chief of staff or the commissar, received us and praised our attitudes. They believed that we hadn't thrown ourselves into the enemy's embrace and betrayed our country, and our task in the future was to confess our illicit love affair. If we confessed well, they would allow us to get married.

But we didn't want to get married. So later they said if we confessed well, they would let me go back to civilization, and Chen Qingyang would get to work in a bigger hospital. So I stayed in my hotel room and wrote confessions for over a month. Nothing interrupted me except the government business that I had to perform. I used carbon copies; the originals I kept, the duplicates I gave to her. We used exactly the same confessions.

After a while, the security comrades came to talk to me, telling me about the big denouncement meeting they were going to hold. All the people who had been investigated by the public security section would have to attend, including speculators, grafters, and all kinds of bad elements. We belonged in the group, but the regimental leaders said that since we were young people, and had good attitudes, we didn't have to go. But people compared their situation with ours, and asked, if everyone who'd been investigated had to be there, why were we being let off? The security comrades were in a fix. So we would have to take part in the meeting. Finally they decided to work on mobilizing us to take part. They told us that public denouncing had an impact on a person's mind, which could prevent us from committing errors in the future. Since there was such an advantage, how could we miss the opportunity? When the meeting day came, several thousand people flooded in from the farm headquarters and the nearby production teams. We stood on the stage with many others. After waiting a long time and hearing quite a few articles of denouncement read, our turn, convicts Wang and Chen, finally came. It turned out that we were loose in morals and corrupted in lifestyle, and what was more, in order to evade thought reform, we had fled into the mountains. Only under the influence of our party's policy did we come down the mountain to abandon darkness for sunlight. Hearing comments like this, our emotions were stirred up, too. So we raised our arms and shouted out the slogans: Down with Wang Er! Down with Chen Qingyang! After this round of public denouncement, we thought we were done with it. But we still had to write confessions because the leaders wanted to read them.

On the back slope of the fifteenth team, Chen Qingyang, seized with an impulse once, said she was going to bear a litter of young for me, but I wasn't interested. Later I thought having babies wasn't a bad idea. But when I mentioned it to her, she changed her mind. And she always thought that it was me who wanted to have sex. She said, If you feel like it, just do it. I don't care. I thought it would be too selfish if it were only for me. So I rarely asked for it. Besides, cultivating the wilderness was very tiring and I didn't have the energy for it. What I could confess was that I fondled her breasts when we rested at the edge of the field.

When we cultivated the wilderness in the dry season, hot air was all around. We didn't sweat at all, but our muscles felt dry and painful. On the hottest days, we could only sleep under a tree, with heads pillowed on bamboo stalks and bodies lying on palm-bark rain capes. I wondered why nobody asked me to confess about the palm-bark rain cape, one of the labor-protection supplies for our farm, and very expensive. I brought two along; one was mine, the other one I picked up conveniently from someone's doorway. I returned neither of them to the farm. Even when I left Yunnan, no one asked me to return the palm-bark rain capes.

During our break at the edge of the field, Chen Qingyang covered her face with a bamboo hat, opened her shirt collar, and immediately fell asleep. I reached in, feeling the beautiful curves. After a while, I unbuttoned a few more buttons, seeing that her skin was pink. Even though she always worked with her clothes on, the sunshine still got through the thin fabric. As for me, working bare to the waist, I had turned as black as a devil.

Chen Qingyang's breasts were two firm scoops, even when she lay back. But the other parts of her body were very slender. She hadn't changed much in twenty years, except that her nipples had grown a little bit bigger and darker. She said the culprit was her daughter. When the child was a newborn, she looked like a pink baby pig. With eyes closed, she swooped down on her mother's nipples sucking with all her might, until her mother became an old woman and she a beautiful young woman, a young version of her mother.

An older woman now, Chen Qingyang had become more sensitive. When we relived our old days in the hotel, she seemed nervous about such subjects. She hadn't been that way before. Back when I hesitated to mention her breasts in the confessions, she said, Just write it down. I said, You'd be exposed then. She said, Let me be exposed. I don't care. She also said her breasts were made this way. It wasn't like she had done something to fake them. As for what other people thought when they heard about them, it wasn't her problem.

After all those years, I just discovered that Chen Qingyang was actually my ex-wife. After we finished our confessions, they wanted us to get married. I thought it was unnecessary. But the leaders said that not getting married would have a very bad influence and insisted that we register. So we registered to get married in the morning and divorced in the afternoon. I thought it hadn't counted. In the confusion they forgot to take our marriage certificate back, and so Chen Qingyang kept one for herself. We used this shabby certificate issued to us twenty years ago to get a double room. Without this, we wouldn't be allowed to stay in the same room. It was different twenty years ago. Twenty years ago they let us stay in the same hotel room to write our confessions, and back then we didn't even have the marriage certificate.

I wrote about what we had done on the back slope. But the regional leaders asked the security comrades to pass on a message to me, saying that I could skip over the irrelevant details. Just move on to the next case. Hearing this, I lost my stubborn-as-a-mule temper: The motherfuckers! Is this a case? Chen Qingyang tried to help me understand: How many people are there in the world? How many times do people do it every day? And how many of them are important enough to be called cases? I said actually they were all cases. It was just that the leaders couldn't check on them all. She said, Well then, just confess. So I confessed: That night, we left the back slope and returned to the scene of the crime.

7

Later I saw Chen Qingyang again. We registered for a room at a hotel, went in together, and then I helped her take off her coat. Chen Qingyang said, Wang Er has become civilized. It meant I had changed a lot. In the old days, I did not just look ferocious, but also acted ferociously.

Chen Qingyang and I committed the crime one more time in the hotel. The room was well heated, and the windows were glazed with tea-colored panes. I sat on the sofa, and she sat in the bed. We chatted for a while, and then the criminal atmosphere began to build. I said, Didn't you want me to see how they sag now? Let me take a look! So she got to her feet and took off her sweater—she had on a flowery shirt underneath. Then she sat back and said, It's still early. After a while, the attendant brought us boiling water. They had keys, so they just came in without even knocking on the door. I asked, What would the attendant say if he came in right in the middle of things? She said she had never gotten caught in the act, but she had heard that the attendant would slam the door shut and curse, Motherfuckers! Disgusting!

Before Chen Qingyang and I escaped into the mountains, I cooked pig feed for a while. At the time I had to tend the fire, chop the pig feed (the so-called pig feed consisted of things like sweet potato vine and water hyacinth), and add chaff and water to the wok all by myself. As I bustled around doing several things at once, the military deputy stood beside me, talking his head off. He went on nagging about how bad I was, and how bad Chen Qingyang was, even asking me to pass the message to my "stinking whore" Chen Qingyang. All of a sudden, I flew into a fury. I grabbed a machete and slashed at a bottle gourd used for storing pumpkin seeds that hung on the beam, cutting it in half. Frightened, the military deputy leaped out of the room. If he had kept scolding, I would have cut his head off. I appeared especially ferocious, because I didn't speak.

Later, in the public security office, I didn't talk much either, even when they were tying me up. So my hands often turned dark blue. Chen Qingyang talked all the time. She would say something like this: Big sister, it hurts! or, Big sister, can you tuck a handkerchief under the rope? There is a handkerchief holding my hair. She cooperated at every point, which was why she suffered much less than I did. We were different in every way.

Chen Qingyang said that back then I wasn't very civilized. When we went back to the public security office, people untied us. The rope left lines of smudge on her shirt, which was because the rope was stored in a kitchen shed and picked up ash from the bottom of woks and bits of firewood. She tried to flick the ashes off with her stiff fingers, but could only do the front, not the back. By the time she wanted to ask me to help her, I had already strode out of the room. She followed out the door, but I had gone pretty far. I walked very fast, never looking back. Because of these things, she didn't love me at all; she didn't even like me.

According to the leaders, what we did on the back slope was not considered a primary offense—except the time that she looked like a koala bear. For example, the thing we did while cultivating the wilderness was just a secondary offense. So I didn't finish my confession. There was actually something more. A hot wind blew really hard at the time and Chen Qingyang slept soundly with her arms under her head. I unbuttoned all the buttons on her shirt so she was half naked. It looked like she had done it herself. The sky was so blue and bright that you could even see blue light in the shadows. All of a sudden, I felt tenderness in my heart, so I bent over her reddened body. I'd forgotten what I did then. When I mentioned this to Chen Qingyang, I thought she'd have forgotten. But she said, "I remember, I remember. I was already awake by that time. You kissed my belly button, right? I was just on the edge—I almost fell in love with you at that moment."

Chen Qingyang said that she had just awakened in time to see my tousled head on her belly, and then she felt a gentle touch on her navel. For a moment she could hardly restrain herself, but she still pretended to sleep, waiting to see what else I would do. But I didn't do anything. I raised my head and looked around. And then I walked away.

My confession says that on that night, we left the back slope and set off for the crime scene. We carried pots and pans on our backs and planned to settle down on the mountain in the south. Over there the soil was so much richer that the grasses on both sides of the road stood as tall as people, unlike the back slope of the fifteenth team where they were about half a foot. The moon shone that night. We even walked on the road for a while. By the time fog rose at daybreak, we had walked twelve miles and went up to the mountain in the south. To be more specific, we arrived at the grassland to the south of Zhang Feng village and the forest wasn't far off. We camped under a huge green tree, picking up two pieces of cow dung to start a fire, and spread a plastic sheet on the ground. Then we took off all our clothes (the clothes were drenched by then), cuddled into each other, wrapped ourselves in three blankets, and then fell asleep. We woke up frozen after an hour. The three layers of blankets were all soaked, and the dung fire had died out, too. Dewdrops fell from the trees in a downpour, and even the drops floating in the air were as big as mung beans. This was in January, the coldest days of the dry season. The shady side of the mountain could be that damp.

Chen Qingyang said when she woke up she heard my teeth chattering like a machine gun by her ear. The upper teeth were clicking against the lower more than once a second. I already had a temperature. Once I caught a cold, it would be hard to recover unless I got a shot. So she sat up and said, Enough. Both of us will get sick this way. Hurry, we have to do the thing. Not wanting to move, I said, Hold on for a bit. The sun is coming out soon. After a few minutes I said, Do you think I have energy to do it now? That was the situation prior to the offense.

The offense went as follows: Chen Qingyang rode my body, up and down; behind her back was a broad expanse of white fog. It didn't feel that cold anymore, and the sound of buffalo bells floated all around. Since Thai people here didn't pen their buffaloes, they would ramble at daybreak. Hung with wooden bells, the buffaloes would make clunking sounds as they walked. A hulk suddenly turned up beside us, with dewdrops dangling from a hairy ear. It was a white buffalo, who turned its head and stared at us with one of its eyes.

A white buffalo's horn can be used to make a knife handle, glittering and crystal clear, very pretty. But its texture is brittle, easy to crack. I used to have a dagger with a white-horn handle that didn't have any cracks, which was very unusual. The blade was also made of excellent materials. Unfortunately public security confiscated it. I asked them to return it to me after my case was cleared. They said they couldn't find it. They didn't return my hunting gun either. Old Guo from the public security section promised shamelessly to buy it, but he only wanted to pay fifty yuan. In the end I got nothing back, not my gun or my knife.

Chen Qingyang and I chatted for a long time before we committed our crime in the hotel room. Finally, she took off her shirt, but still wore her skirt and leather boots. I went over to sit next to her and moved her hair back; some of it had turned gray.

Chen Qingyang had permed her hair. She said she used to have excellent hair and didn't want to perm it. Now it didn't matter anymore. As the assistant head of the hospital, she was very busy and couldn't even find time to wash her hair every day. Other than that, the corners of her eyes and her neck had begun to crease. She said her daughter suggested that she have plastic surgery, but she couldn't find time to do it.

At last she said, OK, now take a look at them. So she started to undo her bra. I wanted to help her, but I couldn't. The clasp was in the front, but I reached around to her back. She said, Looks like you haven't learned what it takes to be bad. And then she turned to let me see her breasts. I looked carefully at them for a while, and gave her my opinion. For some reason, her face blushed a little. She said, Well, you've seen them. What else do you want to do? As she said this, she began to put her bra back on. I said, What's the hurry? Leave them out. She said, What? Still want to study my anatomy? I said, Of course. But let's not rush. We can talk a little longer. The color in her face deepened. She said, Wang Er, you'll never learn how to be good. You'll always be a bastard!

When I was detained in the public security section, Luo Xiaosi came to see me. He leaned on the windowsill and found me tied up like a package. Believing that my case was very serious and I might be shot soon, he tossed a box of cigarettes in from the window and said, Brother Er, just a little gift. Then he burst into tears. Luo Xiaosi was a sentimental man, easily touched. I asked him to light a cigarette and hand it to me through the window. He did as I asked, almost dislocating his shoulder to reach me. After that he asked me what else he could do for me. I said nothing else. I also said, Don't bring a crowd to see me. He promised he wouldn't. After he was gone, a gang of boys climbed up to the window ledge to see me. Right then the cigarette smoke choked me, and with one eye open and the other closed I looked terrible. The leader of the boys couldn't help crying out: Hooligan! I answered back, Your father and mother are hooligans! If they're not hooligans, where did a little hooligan like you come from? The boy grabbed some dirt and flung it at me. After I was released, I went to see the boy's father and said: Today I was in the public security office. I was hog-tied. Your son is young, but he has great ambition. He took the opportunity to fling dirt at me. After hearing this, the man grabbed his son and beat the shit out of the little bastard. I didn't leave until I witnessed the whole episode. When Chen Qingyang heard this, she commented, Wang Er, you're a bastard!

Actually I'm not always a bastard. Now that I have a wife and family, I have learned a lot about how to be good. After finishing the cigarette, I drew her to me, fondled her breasts skillfully for a while, and then wanted to take off her skirt. She said, No rush. Let's talk a little more. Give me a cigarette too. So I lit a cigarette, took a drag, and handed it to her.

Chen Qingyang said on Mount Zhang Feng, when she rode up and down on my body, she looked far and near, and saw nothing but gray, watery fog floating in the air. All of a sudden, she felt very alone, very lonely. Even though a part of me was rubbing inside her body, she still felt sad and lonely. After a while I came back to life and said: Let's switch. Here we go. So I rolled over onto her body. She said, That time, you were a bigger bastard than ever.

When Chen Qingyang said I was a bigger bastard than ever, she meant that I suddenly noticed her feet were cute and pretty. I said, Old Chen, I've decided to be a foot fetishist. Then I raised her legs and started to kiss the soles of her feet. Chen Qingyang lay on the grass with her arms spread out and her hands grabbing the grass, and then she turned her head aside, her hair covering her face, and moaned.

In my confession I wrote: I let go of her legs and parted the hair on her face. She struggled violently to break free, tears rolling down from her eyes, but she didn't slap me. There were two unhealthy red spots on her cheeks. After a while, she no longer struggled and said, You bastard! What are you going to do with me? I said, What's wrong? She smiled and said, Nothing. Keep going. So I raised her legs again. She lay like that motionless, her arms spread out, teeth biting her lower lip without uttering a sound. If I looked at her again, she smiled back. I remember her face was extremely pale, and her hair was especially dark. That's how the whole thing went.

Chen Qingyang said when she lay in the cold rain that time, she felt the chill penetrate every pore. She felt an endless flow of sorrow. Just then a huge surge of orgasm sliced through her body. Cold fog and icy rain both seeped into her body. For a moment she wanted to die. She couldn't stand it; she wanted to cry out. But at the sight of me she changed her mind. There was no man in this world who could make her scream in front of him. She felt disconnected from everyone.

Chen Qingyang told me later that she was deeply troubled every time I made love to her. In the depth of her heart, she wanted to cry out, hug me, and kiss me passionately, but she couldn't bring herself to do it. She didn't want to love other people, not even one. But still, when I kissed the soles of her feet that time, a sharp feeling still bored its way into her heart.

When Chen Qingyang and I made love on Mount Zhang Feng, an old buffalo alongside us watched. Later it lowed and ran away, leaving the two of us alone there. After a long while, the sky gradually lightened and the fog began to disappear from above us. Chen Qingyang's body glistened with dew. I let go of her and rose to my feet, to find that we were actually not far from the village. So I said, Let's go. We left that place and never went back.

8

In my confession, I admitted that Chen Qingyang and I had committed crimes on numerous occasions on Grandpa Liu's back mountain. This was because Grandpa Liu's fields had already been cultivated and didn't need much work. So our life was relatively easy there. And since we didn't have to worry about food and shelter, we thought more about sex. There was nobody else on that part of the mountain, and Grandpa Liu lay on his deathbed. The mountain was either rainy or foggy. Chen Qingyang fastened my belt around her waist, with a knife dangling from it. She wore high boots, and nothing else.

Chen Qingyang told me later that she had made only one friend in her life, and that was me. She said all that happened came about because I talked about great friendship in my small house by the river. A person had to accomplish a few things in life and this was one of them. After that she didn't have deep relationships with other people. It's no fun doing the same things over and over.

I've had a feeling about this all along. So whenever I asked her for sex, I would say, Old pal, how about strengthening our great friendship now? Married couples have a code of ethics to strengthen, and we don't have that, so we can only strengthen our friendship. She said, No problem. How do you want to strengthen it, from the front or from the back? I said, From the back. We were at the edge of the field then. Because it was from the back, we had to spread two palm-bark rain capes on the ground. She knelt on her hands and knees, like a horse, and said,

You'd better hurry. It's time to give Grandpa Liu a shot. I wrote all these things in my confessions, but the leaders wanted me to confess in response to the following:

1. Who is Comrade Strain-thing Eh-thics?
2. What does "strengthening the great friendship" mean?
3. What is strengthening it from the back? And what is strengthening it from the front?

After I cleared things up, the leaders told me not to play word games. Whatever my crimes were, they said, I needed to confess them.

While we were strengthening our great friendship on the mountain, white breath puffed from our mouths. It was not that cold, but very humid. You could grab a handful of air and wring water out of it. Worms wriggled next to our palm-bark rain capes. That piece of land was really rich. Later on, before the corn fully ripened, we picked the ears and ground the kernels in a mortar. The Jingpos in the mountains prepared corn cakes that way, and they weren't bad at all. Storing them in cold water could preserve them for a long time.

As Chen Qingyang crouched on her hands and knees in the cold rain, her breasts felt like cool apples. Her skin all over was as smooth as a piece of burnished marble. After a while I pulled my little Buddha out and ejaculated onto the field. She looked back at this with a surprised and fearful expression. I told her that it would fertilize the land. She said, I know. And a moment later she asked, Will a little Wang Er grow out of the land?—Does this sound like something a doctor would say?

When the rainy season passed, we dressed like Thais and went to Qingping market. As I've already written before, I met a classmate in Qingping. Although I was dressed like a Thai, he still recognized me on sight. I was too tall to be a Thai. He said, Hi, brother Er, where have you been? I said, I'm hopeless at speaking Mandarin. Despite the fact that I tried very hard to speak in a weird accent, it still sounded like the Beijing dialect. That one sentence gave me away.

It was her idea to go back to the farm. Since I myself had decided to go up the mountain, I was determined not to go back. She'd come to the mountains for the sake of our great friendship, so I couldn't refuse to go down the mountain with her. Actually, we could have left anytime, but she didn't want to. She said our current life was fun.

Later Chen Qingyang said life on the mountain was also fun. When cold mist drifted over the mountain, she would tuck a knife into her belt, put on a pair of rain boots, and enter the drizzle. But it's no fun doing the same things over and over. That was why she still wanted to come down the mountain, to put up with the torment of human society.

When Chen Qingyang and I relived our great friendship in the hotel room, we spoke of the time we came down the mountain and reached a junction of roads. There were four byroads at that place, and each of them led in a single direction. East, west, south, north didn't really matter. One led abroad, to an unknown place; one to the interior; one to the farm; and one back to where we came from, and that road also led to Husha. In Husha there were a lot of Ahcang blacksmiths, who had passed on the skill from generation to generation. Though I didn't come from a family of smiths, I could have been a blacksmith. I knew those people very well; they all admired my skill. Ahcang women were all very pretty, their bodies adorned with many bronze bracelets and necklaces and silver coins. That kind of dress fascinated Chen Qingyang, and she wanted to go up to the mountains and become one of them. At the time, the rainy season had just passed, and clouds rose up from every direction. Threads of sunshine flashed in the sky. We could have made any choice and set off in any direction. So I stood at the crossroads for a long time. Later when I was going back to the interior, waiting for the bus by the road, I also had two choices: I could keep waiting, or return to the farm. When I walked along one path, I often thought about things that might happen on another path. Then I would feel confused.

Chen Qingyang once said I was a man of average intelligence but with skillful hands, and very nutty, which all meant something. Her saying my intelligence was only average, I didn't agree with; her saying I was nutty, I couldn't deny because it's a fact; as to my skillful hands, she probably knew that from her own body. My hands are indeed very skillful, which wasn't just shown by how I touched women. My palms are not big, but my fingers are unusually long and able to perform any delicate and complex task. Those Ahcang blacksmiths on the mountain were better than me at forging blades, but for etching designs on a knife no one could match me. So, at least twenty blacksmiths invited us to move in with them. Each suggested that he would forge the blades and I would etch the designs, and we would make a good team. If I had moved in then, I probably would have forgotten how to speak Mandarin.

If I had moved in with an Ahcang big brother, I would be etching designs on Husha knives in that dark, deep blacksmith shop now. In the muddy backyard of his house, there would be a brood of little children, comprised of four combinations:

1. Those produced by Chen Qingyang and me;
2. Those produced by Ahcang big brother and Ahcang big sister;
3. Those produced by Ahcang big sister and me;
4. Those produced by Chen Qingyang and Ahcang big brother.

When Chen Qingyang would come down from the mountain with firewood on her back, she would pull up her clothes, revealing her full and firm breasts, and, without making any distinction, feed one of the babies. If I had returned to the mountains then, that would have happened.

Chen Qingyang said such things wouldn't happen because they didn't happen. What really happened was that we returned to the farm, wrote confessions, and went on denouncement trips. Even though we could have run away at any minute, we never did. That was what really happened.

When Chen Qingyang said I was of average intelligence, she obviously didn't consider my literary talent. Everyone loved to read the confessions I wrote. When I first started writing those things, I was dead set against it. But as I wrote more, I became obsessed, clearly because the things I wrote all happened. Things that really happen have incomparable charm.

I wrote down almost every detail in my confessions except the things that happened below:

On the back mountain of the fifteenth team, after making love in our thatched hut, Chen Qingyang and I went to a creek to play in the water. The water from the mountain had washed away the red soil, exposing the blue clay underneath. We lay on the blue clay to sun ourselves. After I recovered my warmth, my little Buddha stood up again. Since he had been relieved not long before, I was not as eager as a sex maniac. So I lay on my side behind her, pillowed on her long hair and entered her body from behind. Later in the hotel room, we relived our great friendship in the same way.

When Chen Qingyang and I lay on our sides on the blue clay, it was getting dark and the wind had cooled a bit. It felt very peaceful lying together, and sometimes we moved a little. I've heard that dolphins had two ways of doing it, one for procreation and the other for entertainment, which is to say that dolphins also have the great friendship. Chen Qingyang and I were connected, just like a pair of dolphins.

When Chen Qingyang and I lay on the blue clay with our eyes closed, we felt like a pair of dolphins swimming in the sea. It was getting darker and the sunlight gradually reddened. A cloud came over the horizon, pale as countless dead fish bellies turned up and countless dead fish eyes gaping. A current of wind slipped down the mountain without a sound, without a breath, and a sadness in the air filled every space between the sky and the earth. Chen Qingyang shed a lot of tears. She said the scene depressed her.

I still keep the duplicates of my confessions from back then. Once, I showed them to a friend who majored in English and American literature. He said they were all very good, with the charm of Victorian underground novels. As for the details I had cut out, he said it was a good idea to cut them out, because those details destroyed the unity of the story. My friend is really erudite. I was very young when I wrote the confessions and didn't have any learning (I still don't have much learning), or any idea what Victorian underground novels were. What I had in my mind was that I shouldn't be an instigator. Many people would read my confessions. If after reading them they couldn't help screwing damaged goods, that wasn't so bad; but if they learned the other thing, that would be really bad.

I also left out the facts that follow, for the same reason mentioned above. We had committed many errors and deserved execution. But the leaders decided to save us, making me write confessions. How forgiving of them! So I made up my mind that I would only write about how bad we were.

When we lived on Grandpa Liu's back slope, Chen Qingyang made a Thai skirt for herself, disguising herself as a Thai woman so she could go to Qingping on market days. But after putting the skirt on she could barely walk. South of Qingping, we ran into a river. The mountain water was ice-cold, and green as marinated mustard. The water reached to my waist, and the current was very swift. I walked over to her, hoisted her onto my shoulder, went right across the river, and then put her down. Her waist was exactly the width of my shoulder. I remember her face turning deep red then. I said, I could carry you to Qingping and back, faster than your swishy walking. She said, Go take a crap.

A Thai skirt is like a cloth sheath. The hem is only about a foot around. People who know how to wear them can do all kinds of things with them on, including peeing on the street without squatting down. Chen Qingyang said she could never learn that trick. After conducting an observation for a while in Qingping market, she drew the conclusion that if she wanted to disguise herself like someone, she would rather be an Ahcang woman. On the way back, the mountain road was all uphill, and she was exhausted, too. So whenever we needed to jump over a ditch or cross a ridge, she would find a stump, gracefully mount it, and let me carry her.

So on the way home I carried her on my shoulder climbing the hills. The dry season had just arrived, white clouds coasted through the sky, and the sun gave brilliant light. But in the mountains it would drizzle from time to time. The red clay was very slippery. Walking on slabs of red mud was like learning to skate for the first time. So with my right hand locked around her thighs and my left hand carrying the rifle, not to mention the basket on my back, I could hardly manage the slippery incline. All of a sudden, I slipped to the left, and was about to fall into the valley. Fortunately I had a rifle, which I used to hold me up. I tensed my whole body and struggled to keep us from going over. But the idiot picked that moment to give me trouble, flopping around on my back and demanding that I put her down. We almost lost our lives that time.

As soon as I caught my breath, I switched the rifle to my right hand, raised my left hand, and slapped her bottom really hard. Through the layer of thin cloth, it felt unusually smooth. Her bottom was very round. Fuck, I felt terrific. She immediately behaved herself after getting spanked. She became very submissive, not saying another word.

Of course, it was wrong to slap her bottom, but I thought this kind of thing might not be what other damaged goods and their lovers get into. So the incident seemed beside the point and I didn't write about it.

9

When Chen Qingyang and I made love on Mount Zhang Feng, she still had a fair complexion, and the veins in her temples stood out clearly. Later in the mountains she turned dark, but became fair again after she returned to the farm. At the time the army and the local civilians worked together to bolster the border defense, maintenance would dispatch a big tractor every Sunday, taking a load of problem people to labor at a brick kiln. After we laid out the bricks, the tractor would take us to the production teams on the borderline to meet with the propaganda team. Our tractor was loaded with historical antirevolutionaries, thieves, procapitalists, damaged goods, and so on, comprising both class enemies and strayed members of the masses. We finished our job and accepted a round of denouncement on the borderline, so that the border's political safety could be strengthened. Going on those trips would get us free meals from the government, and the armed militiamen would guard us when we squatted and ate. After the meal, Chen Qingyang and I would stand leaning against the tractor. Then a group of old women would come over and look her up and down, concluding that with such white skin, no wonder she was damaged goods.

I once went to the public security office to see Old Guo, asking what they meant by making us go on these trips. He said it was no more than showing the enemies on the other side of the border that we were tough, so they didn't dare invade. The two of us were really not supposed to go, but they couldn't get enough people. We were not good people anyway, so it didn't matter. I said, It's true that going on these denouncement trips is no big deal, but you should stop people from pulling Chen Qingyang's hair. If you piss me off, I'm going to run away to the mountains again. He said he knew nothing about the hair-pulling part and would definitely take care of it. Actually, I'd wanted to go back to the mountains for a long time, but Chen Qingyang said, Forget it, what's the big deal about them pulling my hair?

When we went on the denouncement trip, Chen Qingyang wore one of my student uniforms. It was too big for her, the sleeves would hang halfway over her palms, and raising the collar would cover her cheeks. Later she asked for the shirt. I hear she still has it, but only wears it when she cleans the house and washes the windows. She was an expert at getting denounced. Whenever she heard our names called, she would take out a pair of clean "Liberation-brand" shoes from her backpack, tied together with a hemp string, hang them around her neck, and wait to step onto the stage.

Chen Qingyang said after she took a shower at home, she put on that shirt of mine as a bathrobe. Then she showed her daughter how she was denounced back then, how she had to stick out her bottom, and sometimes even had to lift her face to let people see her, the way you dance the samba. The child would ask, What about my dad? Chen Qingyang said, Your dad did the airplane stance. The kid giggled, thinking it was very funny.

When I heard this, I felt very uncomfortable. In the first place, I didn't take the airplane position. At the denouncement meeting, two little Sichuanese escorted me. They were very polite, and always apologized first, Brother Wang, forgive us. Then they pulled back my arms. The people who escorted her were two little bitches from the propaganda team. They not only dragged her by the arms but also pulled her hair. From what she said, it seemed like people treated me worse than her. That was unfair to the two little Sichuanese; in the second place, I'm not her daughter's father. After they finished denouncing us, it would be performance time for the propaganda team. So they ran us off the stage and into the tractor, to drive us back to the farm headquarters the same night. Every time we returned from our denouncement trip, Chen Qingyang would get horny.

We returned to the farm to be criticized and to go on the denouncement trips. But it varied. Sometimes, the regimental commander even invited us to his house, chatting about the errors that we had made. He said he'd made this kind of error himself. Then he would discuss his prostate gland with Chen Qingyang. I would find an excuse to leave them, unless he asked me to fix his watch. Sometimes they treated us very badly, two trips a week. Then the political commissar would say, people like Wang Er and Chen Qingyang, we must denounce. Otherwise, if everyone runs away to the mountains, what will happen to our farm? Honestly, there was some truth in what the commissar said, and besides, he didn't have a prostate problem. That was why Chen Qingyang didn't throw away the pair of worn-out shoes; they always came in handy. After a while, they didn't ask us to go on the denouncement trips anymore. One day, the commissar went out for a meeting. The regimental commander talked to the military affair office and let me go back to the midland cities.

The denouncement trips got started like this: The traditional entertainment in the area was denouncing damaged goods. In the busy season for farming, everyone was exhausted. And the team leader would say, Let's have some entertainment tonight—denouncing damaged goods. But how they entertained, I never got the chance to see. When they denounced damaged goods, they always kicked the bachelors out. Besides, those damaged goods usually had faces as dark as the bottom of a wok and baggy breasts that drooped way down. I didn't want to see them anyway.

Later on, a large number of military cadres came to take over our farm and ordered the denouncing of damaged goods to stop, since the custom didn't conform to party policy. But during the soldier-civilian border-building period, they gave a counterorder allowing the denouncing of damaged goods. The regiment ordered us to report to the propaganda team, to prepare for the denouncement. I wanted to escape to the mountains right away, but Chen Qingyang didn't want to come with me. She said she was obviously the most beautiful of the damaged goods denounced locally. When she was denounced, people came to see her from several production teams nearby, which made her very proud.

When the regiment forced us to take part in the propaganda team's activities, they briefed the propaganda team as follows: our problem was a nonantagonistic contradiction within the people, that is to say, our crimes weren't flagrant and party policy should be observed. But they also said: if the masses became really angry about us, asking to denounce us more vigorously, then proceed flexibly. It turned out the masses got very angry whenever they saw us. The leader of the propaganda team was the regimental commander's man, and his personal relationship with us wasn't bad. So he came to our hotel room to consult with us, Might we increase Doctor Chen's discomfort? Chen Qingyang said, No problem. Next time she would hang a pair of worn-out shoes around her neck. But the masses were still not satisfied. He had no choice but to make Chen Qingyang even more uncomfortable. Finally he said, We are all sensible people. I don't need to say more. You two must excuse me further.

On the denouncement trips, Chen Qingyang and I always hid behind banana trees at first. They were at the back of the stage. When our turn approached, she would rise to her feet, take all the pins out of her hair, hold them in her mouth, and replace them one by one. Then she would turn up her collar, pull down her sleeves, and put her hands behind her back, waiting to be tied up.

Chen Qingyang said they used bamboo rope or coir rope to tie her, which always made her hands swell. So she brought a cotton rope from home she used for hanging her clothes. People complained that women were not easy to tie up because they were plump and curvy, and the rope wouldn't stay on. Then, while a pair of big hands gripped her wrists from behind, another pair of hands tied her tightly, binding her into the loops of the five-petal knot.

Later they escorted her out. Someone would grab her hair from behind, making it impossible for her to look sideways, or lower her head. So she could only tilt her head to the side slightly, to see the crystalline light of the gas lamps. Sometimes she would straighten her head, see some unfamiliar face, and smile at the person. Then she would think, This is a really strange world. What's going on here, she didn't understand at all.

What she did understand was that she was damaged goods now. The rope that bound her was like a straitjacket. Now the curves of her body were completely on display. She noticed all the jutting out at the crotches of the men at the meeting. She knew it was because of her. But why it happened, she didn't understand at all.

Chen Qingyang said when she went on these denouncement trips, they always grabbed her hair and forced her to look around. For their convenience, she combed her hair into two parts and fastened each with rubber bands, so they could hold her wrist with one hand and grab her hair with another. In this way, she was steered into seeing everything, and everything flew into her heart. But she didn't understand anything. Yet she was happy because she did all that people wanted her to do. The rest had nothing to do with her. That was the way she played the role of damaged goods on the stage.

After they finished denouncing us, it was time for the propaganda team to perform. Of course, we were not allowed to watch the performance, so they threw us into the tractor and drove us back to the farm the same night. The driver, anxious to go home to sleep, already had the tractor running. We didn't even have time to untie Chen Qingyang, and I had to carry her to the tractor. Then we got bumped around in the tractor, and since it was pitch-black, I still couldn't untie her. After we arrived at headquarters, I simply carried her back to our hotel room, patiently untying her in the light. By this time Chen Qingyang's face would have a drunken flush and she'd say, Can we strengthen our great friendship now? I can't wait a second longer.

Chen Qingyang said she felt like a gift at that moment, waiting to be unwrapped. So her heart swelled with joy. She had finally liberated herself from all worries; she no longer needed to figure out why she was damaged goods, what damaged goods were, and other baffling questions such as: why we'd come here, what we were doing here, and so forth. Now she put herself in my hands.

At the farm, every time we returned from our denouncement trips, Chen Qingyang would be sure to ask to strengthen our great friendship. We always strengthened it on the desk, which I also used to write my confessions. The height was just right. She looked like a koala on that desk, and, in waves of orgasm, often couldn't help screaming. The light in our room was off then, so I couldn't see her face. Our back window was always open, and a steep slope lay behind the hotel. People often poked their heads in to look around, and those heads appearing on the windowsill looked like crows perching on tree limbs. On the desk I always kept some mountain pears, so hard that no human teeth could bite them, only pigs could eat them. Sometimes she would pick one up and fling it out over my shoulder. She never missed the target, and the person struck would roll down the slope. I didn't enjoy these things. The sperm I finally ejaculated was ice-cold. To tell you the truth, I was afraid of stoning someone to death. Matters like this might have been included in the confessions, but I was afraid others might find out that I continued to commit offenses during the investigation and double the penalty.

10

When we relived our great friendship later in the hotel room, we talked about all kinds of things. We talked about everything we could have done back then, the confessions I wrote, and even the little Buddha of mine. As soon as the thing heard people talking about him, he became excited and began to stir. So I concluded: back then they'd wanted to hammer us but failed. I was still as hard as ever. For the sake of our great friendship, I would even run three times around the block, bare assed. A person like me never cares much about saving face. After all, that was my golden age, even though I was considered a hooligan. I knew a lot of people there, including the nomads in caravans, the old Jingpos living on the mountains, and so on. When you mentioned Wang Er who knew how to fix watches, everyone knew who he was. I could sit with them by the fire and drink the kind of wine that only costs twenty fen for half a gallon. I could drink a lot. I was very popular there.

Other than those people, the pigs in the farm also liked me. That was because when I fed them, I used three times more bran than others did. Because of that I fought with the mess chief. I said, at least our pigs should have enough food. I always had a lot of friendship, and would have liked to share it with everyone. Since they didn't want my friendship, I unloaded all of it on Chen Qingyang.

The strengthening of our great friendship that Chen Qingyang and I did while in the hotel room was of the recreational sort. I pulled out once in the middle of it and found my little Buddha smeared with blood. She said, An older woman's insides get a bit thin, don't push too hard. She also said she'd stayed in the south so long that her hands cracked when she came to the north. The quality of skin cream had declined and it was no use putting it on her hands. After saying this, she took out a small bottle of glycerin and applied some to my little Buddha. Then we did it from the front so we could keep talking. I felt like a wedge for splitting wood, lying between her widely opened legs.

In the lamplight, the network of fine lines on Chen Qingyang's face looked like pieces of golden thread. I kissed her mouth, and she didn't object—that is to say her lips were soft and parted. She hadn't let me kiss her mouth before, only letting me kiss the line between her chin and her neck. She said this would arouse her. Then we continued to talk about things past.

Chen Qingyang said that was also her golden age. Even though people called her damaged goods, she was innocent. She was still innocent now. After hearing this, I laughed. But she said, what we're doing now doesn't count as a sin. We had a great friendship, ran away, went on denouncement trips together, and now that we met again after twenty years' separation, of course she would open her legs to let me crawl in. So even if it were considered a sin, she didn't know where the sin lay. More importantly, she had no knowledge of this sin.

Then once again, she began to breathe heavily. Her face turned scarlet, her legs locked me tightly, and her body beneath me tensed while again and again muffled screams came through her clenched teeth. Only after a long while did she relax. Then she said it was not bad at all.

After the "not bad at all," she still said it was no sin. Because she was like Socrates, ignorant of everything. Even though she had lived more than forty years, the world before her eyes still appeared miraculous and new. She didn't know why they dispatched her to a desolate place like Yunnan, nor did she know the reason for letting her return; she didn't know why they accused her of being damaged goods and escorted her to the stage to be denounced, nor could she figure out why they said she was not damaged goods and removed the confessions she had written from her file. There were all kinds of explanations for these things, but she understood none of them. She was so ignorant that she had to be innocent. So it is written in all the law books.

Chen Qingyang said, People live in this world to suffer torment until they die. Once you figure this out, you'll be able to bear everything calmly. To explain how she came to this realization, we need to go all the way back to the time I returned from the hospital and left for the mountains from her place. I asked her to come to see me and she hesitated for a long time. When she finally decided and walked through the hot noon air to my thatched hut, many beautiful images went through her mind during those moments. Then she entered the thatched hut and saw my little Buddha sticking up like an ugly instrument of torture. She cried out then and abandoned all hope.

Chen Qingyang said, twenty years earlier, on a winter day, she walked into her courtyard. She had on a cotton coat then, and climbed across the threshold clumsily. A grain of sand suddenly got into her eye. It was so painful and the cold wind was so cutting that her tears kept rolling down. She couldn't bear it and wept, as if she were in her little bed trying to cry herself awake. This was an old habit born with her, deeply rooted, that we are wailing our way from one dream into another—this was the extravagant hope that we all have.

Chen Qingyang said that when she went to look for me, golden flies danced in the woods. The wind blew from every direction, penetrating her clothes and climbing her body. The place I lived could be called an empty mountain without a human trace. The burning sunlight dropped from the heights like shattered bits of mica. Beneath her thin, white smock, she had stripped off all her underwear. At that moment her heart, too, was full of extravagant hope. After all, it was also her golden age, even though she was called damaged goods.

Chen Qingyang said, when she went into the mountains to look for me, she climbed over a bare hill. Wind blew in from below and caressed her sensitive parts. And the desire she felt then was as unpredictable as wind. It dispersed just like the wild mountain wind. She thought about our great friendship, thought about how I hurried down the mountain. She also remembered my head of tousled hair; how directly I stared at her when I proved she was damaged goods. She felt she needed me, and we could become one, female and male in a single body, just as when she crawled over the threshold as a child and felt the wind outside. The sky was so blue, the sunshine so bright, and there were pigeons flying around in the sky. The whistling of those pigeons you would remember for the rest of your life. She wanted to talk to me at that moment, just as she longed to merge with the outside world, to dissolve into the sky and the earth. If there were only one person—only her—in this world, she would feel too lonely.

Chen Qingyang said, when she went to my little thatched hut, she thought about everything except the little Buddha. That thing was too ugly to appear in her musing. Chen Qingyang wanted to wail then, but she couldn't cry out, as if someone were choking her. This is the so-called truth. The truth is that you can't wake up. That was the moment she finally figured out what the world was made of; and the next moment she made up her mind: she stepped forward to accept the torment. She felt unusually happy.

Chen Qingyang also said, just then, she once again remembered the moment she cried without restraint in the doorway. She cried and cried, but couldn't awaken from crying, and the agony was undiminished. She cried for a long time, but she didn't want to give up hope, not until twenty years later when she faced the little Buddha. It was not the first time that she faced the little Buddha. But before then she didn't believe there was such a thing in the world.

Chen Qingyang said, facing this ugly thing, she remembered our great friendship. When she was in the university, she had a female classmate who was as ugly as a devil (or to put it in these terms, she looked like my little Buddha). But the girl insisted on sharing a bed with her. What was more, when everyone fell fast sleep, the girl would kiss her mouth and fondle her breasts. To tell the truth, she didn't have this particular hobby, but tolerated it for the sake of their friendship. Now, here was this thing baring its teeth and unsheathing its claws, and wanting exactly the same thing. Then let it be satisfied, which in addition can be a way to make friends. So she stepped forward, burying its ugliness deep inside her. She felt unusually happy.

Chen Qingyang said until then she still believed she was innocent, even after she ran away into the heart of the mountains and strengthened our great friendship almost every day. She said this wouldn't prove she was bad at all because she didn't know why my little Buddha and I wanted to do this. She did it for our great friendship. Great friendship is a promise. Keeping a promise is certainly no sin. She had promised to help me in every respect. But I spanked her bottom in the midst of the mountains, which completely tarnished her innocence.

11

I wrote confessions for a long time. The leaders always said that I didn't confess thoroughly enough and needed to continue. So I thought I would have to spend the rest of my life confessing. Finally, Chen Qingyang wrote a confession without letting me see it and turned it into the public security office. After that, no one asked us to write confessions or go on denouncement trips anymore. What was more, Chen Qingyang began to distance herself from me. I lived a listless existence for a while and went back to the interior alone. What she wrote in the end, I hadn't a clue.

I lost everything when I came back from Yunnan: my gun, my knife, and my tools. I gained one thing: a bulging file of confessions. From then on, wherever I went, people would know that I was a hooligan. One benefit I got was that I returned to the city earlier than the other city students. But what was the good of returning earlier? I still had to be reeducated in the countryside near Beijing.

When I went to Yunnan, I had brought a full set of tools with me: wrench, small vise, and so on. Besides a set of fitter's tools, I also had a set of watchmaker's tools. I used them to fix watches while living on Grandpa Liu's back slope. Even though the mountain was empty and lonely, some bands of horsemen passed by from time to time. Some of them let me appraise the smuggled watches. Whatever the value I suggested, that would be the price, the watch would be worth that much. Of course I didn't do it for free. So I lived quite comfortably in the mountains. If I hadn't come down, I'd be a millionaire by now.

As for that double-barreled shotgun, it was a treasure as well. It turned out that the locals didn't value carbines and rifles much, but the double-barreled shotgun was a rarity to them. The barrel was so heavy, plus there were two. I could really scare people off with it. Otherwise we would have been robbed long ago. Nobody wanted to rob me or Grandpa Liu, but they might want to take Chen Qingyang away. As for my knife, I always fastened it on a cowhide belt, and the cowhide belt was always fastened around Chen Qingyang's waist. She wouldn't take it off even when she was sleeping or making love to me. She thought it was charming to carry a knife with her. So you can say that the knife actually belonged to Chen Qingyang. As I mentioned before, both the knife and gun were confiscated by the public security office. I didn't bring my tools with me when I came down the mountains; I left them on the mountain in case things didn't go smoothly. By the time I went back to Beijing, I was in a hurry and didn't have time to fetch the tools. That was how I was reduced to a complete zero.

I told Chen Qingyang that I could never figure out what she wrote in her last confession. She said she couldn't tell me right then. She wanted to wait until we said goodbye to each other. She was going back to Shanghai the next day. She asked me to see her off at the train station.

Chen Qingyang was different from me in every respect. After daybreak, she took a cold shower (the hot water had run out), and then began to dress up. From underwear to outfit, she was a perfumed lady. I, on the other hand, was a genuine local hooligan from underwear to outfit. No wonder people took the confessions out of her file but left mine. That is to say, her hymen had grown back. As for me, I never had that thing anyway. Besides that, I also committed the crime of instigation. We had committed many errors together and since she didn't know what her sin was, it had to be counted as mine.

We checked out and walked in the street. Now I began to think that the last confession of hers must be extremely obscene. Those who read our confessions were people with stone hearts and high political consciousness. If they couldn't bear reading it, it had to be pretty bad. Chen Qingyang said, in that confession, she wrote nothing but her true sin.

Chen Qingyang said that by her true sin she meant the incident on Mount Qingping. She was being carried on my shoulder then, wearing the Thai skirt that bound her legs tightly together, and her hair hung down to my waist. The white cloud in the sky hurried on its journey, and there were only two of us in the midst of mountains. I had just smacked her bottom; I spanked her really hard. The burning feeling was fading. After that I cared about nothing else but continuing to climb the mountain.

Chen Qingyang said that moment she felt limp all over, so she let go of herself, hanging over my shoulder. That moment she felt like a spring vine entangling a tree, or a young bird clinging to its master. She no longer cared about anything else, and at that moment she had forgotten everything. At that moment she fell in love with me, and that would never change.

At the train station, Chen Qingyang told me when she submitted this confession, the regimental commander read it immediately. And after he finished reading his face was red all over, just like your little Buddha. People who read this confession later all blushed too, like the little Buddha. Afterward the public security people approached her several times, asking her to rewrite it. But she said, This is what really happened. Not a word should be changed. They had no choice but to place it into her file.

Chen Qingyang said, admitting this amounts to admitting all her sins. When she was in the public security office, they showed her all kinds of confessions, just to let her know what she couldn't write in her confession. But she insisted on writing in this way. She said that the reason that she wanted to write about it was because it was worse than anything else she had done. She admitted before that she opened her legs; now she added that the reason she had done it was because she liked it. Doing something is very different from liking it. The former warranted going on denouncement trips; and the latter warranted being torn apart by five running horses or being minced by thousands of knives. But no one had the power to tear us apart with five horses, so they had no choice but to set us free.

After Chen Qingyang told me this, the train roared away. From that moment on, I never saw her again.

East Palace, West Palace

1

The setting of this story is a small southern city in whose central district is a small park, and in the park is a police station. One morning, a young policeman from the station comes to work, walking into the huge main office. Before he enters the office, he hears cheering and laughter coming from inside; after he enters he encounters a silence directed at him. During this stretch of silence, a big brown envelope is placed into his hand after several exchanges. The policeman who hands him the envelope adds: Xiao Shi, save the stamps for me. Judging by the handwriting and the colorful Hong Kong stamps on the envelope, Xiao Shi immediately knows who sent it. In that room, under the gaze of those people, it would be better not to open the envelope right then of course. But he can't bear to wait and opens it. There is nothing in the envelope but a thin book, not even a letter slipped between the pages, or a line of handwriting on the title page. After leafing through the book, Xiao Shi feels disappointed. Just then he catches sight of the words printed on the title page, "For my lover." Seeing this line, he gives a long sigh, as if something has fallen into place. Carefully he runs his fingers over the words. Then he locks the book in his drawer and goes out.

As for the book, we should add that it came from Ah-Lan. His name was written on the envelope, printed in the book, and the book itself was written by Ah-Lan. Everyone in the room saw that Xiao Shi received a book from Ah-Lan, how he hurriedly searched through the book, how he eagerly examined the words on the title page and how he touched the words—all of this took place quietly under everyone's watchful eyes. The people in the room find Xiao Shi sentimental and disgusting. Most people would feel contented after witnessing this. If there were one person who thought it wasn't enough, who had to open Xiao Shi's drawer, take out the book, and pass it around the room, it would have been Xiao Shi's wife Dian Zi. She actually does this. She takes out the book, carefully searches through it, and finally finds the inscription on the title page. She exposes the part of Xiao Shi that he doesn't want anyone to see. Of course, it isn't a sensible thing to do, but Dian Zi is far from sensible.

Xiao Shi receives a book from Ah-Lan and feels very excited. His heart pounds wildly because of it, his face blushes because of it, and his hands tremble because of it. He doesn't want to stay in the office to let others see him, so he runs out. This mental state is what we call "love." He goes to the public toilet first, which is a meeting place for gay men. He runs into several people there of that circle. They pay special attention to his expression. He doesn't want their attention, so he rushes out and wanders in the park. But everyone he meets in the park looks at him with special attention. He thinks all this attention can't mean anything good. He carefully avoids the stares and goes to a corner of the park. There is a bench in this spot, and a year ago, Ah-Lan sat right on the bench. At this moment of this hour, Xiao Shi also sits on the bench, burying his face in his hands. It has been some time since Ah-Lan left him. He can't see him, can't feel his body or smell his scent. But a book from him can strike him like lightning. He never had these feelings. Xiao Shi tells himself: This might be what people call "love."

2

Meanwhile, Ah-Lan lives in a faraway place, in a white room. The room is very spacious, with only a mattress placed on the floor under the window. The day is scorching hot, and he has nothing on but a white terrycloth blanket wrapped around his waist. On the mattress lies the book he wrote, exactly the same as the one he sent to Xiao Shi. In front of him are a large cola bottle and an empty cup. For him, the small park, the people in the park, and the rest have all become the past. Of course he remembers the people, and the despair. It had been like passing through a long, crowded corridor all alone, the people blocking your way dodged without saying a word, and all the remarks came from behind your back. It had been like sleeping naked on a sheet with countless bedbugs crawling beneath it. That was the kind of despair that had pursued him from behind; the kind that approached head-on was a young policeman with bared fangs and unsheathed claws, who insulted him, mistreated him, but whom Ah-Lan loved. The young policeman was Xiao Shi.

As for the young policeman, we should add that he was extremely good-looking, well kempt with an unaffected, charming manner. As when you see a beautiful girl at the grocery and wonder how someone like her came to be there, so it was with that young policeman at the police station in the park. The park was a gay meeting place, where they talked about men the way men talked about women. So the young policeman was the heartthrob of the park—of course, he himself didn't know this. When he went to the public toilet—he had to go there of course, because there was only one public toilet in that park, and a heartthrob had to go to the toilet, too—all of them would poke their heads out from behind the partitions. It would be hard to imagine a man following a heartthrob of the opposite sex into a public toilet, to get a vision of her sitting on the toilet (let alone squatting over a pit), but a gay man would do it to his heartthrob.

3

As for the young policeman, we know that every time he worked the night shift, he would arrest a gay man to keep him company. One night, he caught Ah-Lan on a long park bench. At the time Ah-Lan was sitting on another man's lap and necking with the man. All of a sudden, a beam from a flashlight lit them up, stunning them into wide-eyed, open-mouthed surprise. The young policeman behind the light said, Hey, you two, that's really a new one. Ah-Lan stood up then, and the other man ran off. The young policeman strode forward, grabbed his wrist, and said, You're not going anywhere. Ah-Lan didn't get caught very often, so he felt thunderstruck, his eyes staring and his mouth gaping. The young policeman swept the light over his face and said, You look very familiar. Do you come here often? Ah-Lan couldn't answer his question because he was too nervous. The young policeman said, Take a little trip with me. He took out a set of handcuffs and said, Should I have you wear these? Ah-Lan stammered, What? The young policeman said, Do you want to run away? Ah-Lan said, no . . . no. Then we won't need these, the young policeman said. That's the way it should be. The monk may flee, but his temple remains. He tucked the handcuffs into his belt and pulled Ah-Lan along with him. As he looked back on it, the fear vanished and Ah-Lan spoke of how beautifully that night began. Xiao Shi's grip made his heart race. And how excited he was when Xiao Shi was going to put handcuffs on him. The feelings flustered him.

4

As the young policeman pulled Ah-Lan along, walking on the avenue, he educated Ah-Lan. The interesting part is that the education started with Xiao Shi persuading Ah-Lan not to be too afraid, not to tremble so much. He had committed an error, but the error wasn't big, "You haven't robbed a bank or waylaid someone for the purpose of rape," so Xiao Shi didn't want to make too much trouble for Ah-Lan. We know that he detained Ah-Lan for amusement (we'll return to this later). If Ah-Lan was scared into a slimy heap, then it wouldn't be any fun.

Much later, when Ah-Lan recalled that night, he felt that the way Xiao Shi held his hands while walking was like an adult dragging a naughty boy. That is, the former walked straight ahead, and the latter walked sideways. However, he liked to imagine it more as a handsome boy dragging his naughty girlfriend. This, of course, was the result of his preference.

The young policeman talked about Ah-Lan's error this way, "I know all about you people's business . . . ten slits are not as good as one hole to you, right? Close is close enough, why be so picky? If there's a slit, take a slit. We're still at the beginning stage of socialism, let's not learn the advanced stuff from foreigners." Ah-Lan was shocked to hear this and said, "This isn't about slits or holes. . . ." But the young policeman interrupted him rudely, Don't talk crap to me, I don't want to hear it. Much later, when Ah-Lan recalled these words, he felt the rude, ignorant remarks of the young policeman were not only interesting, but even lovely.

5

That night, when the young policeman pulled Ah-Lan along in the park, Ah-Lan stealthily reached for Xiao Shi's behind, caressing his buttocks. Perhaps any naughty girl would caress her good-looking boyfriend, but he went a little too far. Ah-Lan's hands were extremely expressive, and could touch in a variety of ways. Gradually, the young policeman couldn't get himself to move. As they arrived under the streetlights, the young policeman loosened his grip, and Ah-Lan slowed his footsteps and gradually separated himself from the policeman. Finally he stopped under the streetlights and the young policeman walked away by himself, farther and farther, never turning around until he disappeared into the curtain of the night. That was how Ah-Lan escaped from him that night. However, when he thought about it later, he felt infinite remorse. Obviously, he should have gone to the police station with Xiao Shi, listened to his reprimands, and kept him company for the night. Besides, his reaching out to caress the young policeman's behind was vulgar behavior of an unparalleled sort; and running away really went against his true intent. Ah-Lan blamed it on the inferior nature of the vulgar male. He himself ruined the romantic mood of that night.

Ah-Lan believed the beauty of love didn't depend on your lover but on yourself: it depended on your own gentleness and meekness. So even if you had the loveliest lover, if you yourself weren't gentle and meek, then it couldn't be counted as a beautiful love. For this reason, Ah-Lan arranged to sit in front of Xiao Shi again later, and he arranged it completely on purpose. But this time Xiao Shi was not only short-tempered, but also interested in settling their old score, which was exactly what Ah-Lan expected.

6

In the evening, Xiao Shi returns to his office in the police station, turns on the desk lamp, and leafs through the book. He hoped the book would deal with their love, but it turns out to be a historical novel, which disappoints him very much. Whatever the book is he would read it because it was written by Ah-Lan. But he would read it with disappointment. Now the real obstacle to his reading is Ah-Lan himself, or to put it another way, the various memories of Ah-Lan.

A year ago, Ah-Lan sat on the park bench. He wore a purple silk shirt, which stood out distinctly in the park. In Xiao Shi's eyes, his appearance was too flamboyant, and besides, he felt the way Ah-Lan looked at him was strange also. Recalling Ah-Lan's behavior the other day, a wish for revenge rose in Xiao Shi's heart, so he arrested him and took him to the police station.

Xiao Shi ordered Ah-Lan to squat at the base of the wall. Squatting on his left was an art professor, and on his right a construction worker, three of them altogether. The professor on his left had bad breath, and the construction worker on his right was sweaty and smelly, so the smell wasn't much better than the public toilet. The rule here was to make them take the lowest squatting position, that is, to squat like they were shitting, with their hands resting on their knees and their heads hanging forward. Ah-Lan thought the posture inelegant and constantly tried to raise his center of gravity—more accurately, his bottom—and rest it on his calves, but the policeman shouted for him to stop. They were made squat this way so they could think about their errors, but normal people would only think about shitting while squatting like this. That was how the nature of their errors could be determined—their sort of errors were very dirty, and other ways of squatting didn't represent that degree of dirtiness, didn't suit the nature of their errors, and so were forbidden. That was the reason Ah-Lan had to squat that way.

Ah-Lan was in despair before he was taken to the station. After squatting for a while, he got over the mood because his backside hurt, his thighs hurt, and he longed to stand up, so he was no longer in despair. The professor squatting beside him was an older person, and soon it became too much for him and he let out a kind of faint moaning. On the other hand, the construction worker felt pretty good, because he was used to squatting, had something to do, and didn't feel bored. The thing that kept him occupied was rubbing grime in pellets down from his ribs. They squatted behind a policewoman's chair (the policewoman was Dian Zi), which annoyed her. She especially disliked the construction worker's grime-rubbing, so she gave him a piece of paper and told him to rub the grime onto it. But after doing that, she still felt disgusted, so she hurried out, found the young policeman, and told him to get rid of those people. "Spare me the disgust of their squatting here." She spoke in the tone she used to give orders. After saying this, she walked away, demanding that none of these disgusting objects, which included Ah-Lan, be around when she returned. So the young policeman acted on her decree; he told the construction worker to stand up, slapped him twice, fined him, and let him leave. Then he told the professor to stand up, gave him an instructional talk, and let him leave. The aforementioned pair were both gay, and both got caught exhibiting "behavior," and the construction worker even exhibited extorting behavior. All this showed in the young policeman's words. (The young policeman said, What did you do? Would I arrest you for doing nothing? Cut the crap, this is your fine . . . etc. When he spoke to the construction worker, he didn't use the same tone he would use to reprimand children.)

In the young policeman's talk, he emphasized the professor's age and status to prod his sense of shame, but he ignored Ah-Lan. Then he asked his wife to return to her seat, and the latter said grumpily, Why is there one left? As to Xiao Shi's request that she bear with it, her answer was, I don't want to! Finally, she ended up sitting in the young policeman's seat, and the young policeman left. Then the policemen coming in and going out asked her who the man squatting by the corner was, she said, He's Xiao Shi's friend. I hear he's called Ah-Lan. They said, Ah-Lan, I've heard of him. They also said, Xiao Shi is working the night shift. It looks like Xiao Shi is saving him for a chat during the night shift. Some even said, Hope Xiao Shi won't do Ah-Lan. Ah-Lan isn't an ordinary type—they said Ah-Lan is very sexy (they were joking of course). The policewoman stuck out her chest and said with great confidence, He wouldn't dare!

All these conversations went on in front of Ah-Lan, but they all considered Ah-Lan a nonentity, or they wouldn't have made the off-color remarks. It caused Ah-Lan to forget his aching behind and return to his despair—that is, he squatted back dispiritedly.

7

From the heterosexual perspective, especially the policemen's, the homosexuals who got arrested were like caged monkeys. Xiao Shi viewed Ah-Lan the same way. As it got dark, the young policeman, Xiao Shi, made a bowl of instant noodles for himself, while Ah-Lan sat on the ground. Without looking at him, the young policeman said, I didn't give you permission to sit. Ah-Lan squatted. After a while, Ah-Lan arched his back to stand up. The young policeman said, I didn't give you permission to stand up either. Ah-Lan squatted back down, in the shitting position. Then Xiao Shi said, in the tone of a kindergarten teacher, Hey, you do what I tell you. The young policeman finished his noodle soup, made a cup of hot tea for himself, gave a big, lazy stretch, then cast a glance at Ah-Lan, and said, Now you can stand up. So Ah-Lan rose to his feet, and rubbed his knees. Then the young policeman seated himself behind the desk, half-reclining in his chair, with his legs comfortably spread out and said, Come here. When Ah-Lan began to walk over, he added, Take a chair with you. Ah-Lan grabbed a chair, walked to the middle of the room, put the chair down, and sat on it. The two of them began to look at each other. The long night started this way.

At the beginning of that long night, Xiao Shi told Ah-Lan, You son of a bitch had better say something. The latter then said, I'm gay. He also added that everyone's life had a subject, and his subject was homosexuality. Xiao Shi's subject back then was anti-homosexuality, but he could appreciate this kind of directness.

But when Xiao Shi asked him what kind of gay he was, he got quiet. Now a year later, Xiao Shi sits in front of his desk and holds Ah-Lan's book in his hand, and of course he now knows the reason Ah-Lan didn't answer his question was because he loved him. That was the kind of gay he was.

Xiao Shi opens the book and browses the contents—he hoped the book would talk about their love, but it is a historical novel. Still, he would read the book because it was written by Ah-Lan. He would read it with extremely complicated feelings, because the book had no connection to him. Time stops right at the instant that he is about to start reading but hasn't.

8

Ah-Lan said that the long night started this way:

In a stretch of silence, Ah-Lan whispered (his voice was barely audible): Slits are socialism, and holes are capitalism.

The young policeman couldn't believe his own ears: Speak louder. I didn't hear you.

Ah-Lan: Slits are proletarian, and holes are bourgeois.

The young policeman fought back his laughter and said, Louder.

Ah-Lan raised his voice and shouted, Slits are socialism, and holes are capitalism; slits are proletarian, and holes are bourgeois.

The young policeman gestured for him to come closer with a smile, as if he were going to whisper something to him, but instead he slapped Ah-Lan hard.

The slap knocked Ah-Lan to the ground. The young policeman calmed down and said: Get up. After Ah-Lan got up, he then said: Sit down. When Ah-Lan sat down, he cleared his throat and said, "What we're discussing isn't a matter of slits and holes."

Ah-Lan smiled.

Then after a long pause, the young policeman suddenly laughed, and said, Now we're even. What's the fun in sitting like this? Say something, you son of a bitch. At that moment he looked less like a policeman than a mischievous teenager. Later when Ah-Lan sits on his mattress, he says to Xiao Shi's picture, I recall these things not because I want to remember your faults, but to show how I fell in love with you, and why I love you.

9

The major event that occurred that night was: Ah-Lan confessed his personal history to Xiao Shi. This was because the weather was so hot that people couldn't sleep before midnight, and also because there were a lot of mosquitoes in the police station. In short, when Xiao Shi worked the night shift, he would always arrest a homosexual to interrogate, and order them to confess their "activities," so he could kill time and amuse himself. Ah-Lan was the one arrested that night. What he confessed wasn't just his "activities," so what happened that night wasn't just killing time and amusement.

When Ah-Lan stood up from the ground, his legs didn't seem to exist. After a while, they began to hurt and tingle. But he tried his best not to think about things that would drag him down. Now Xiao Shi was sitting right in front of him. He was his dream lover, and also his slave driver. . . . After some hesitation, Ah-Lan began to speak. What he had in mind was that he would tell everything.

On that long night, Ah-Lan confessed about himself this way: "When I was little, I always stayed in the house. There were white walls and a gray concrete floor in the house, I always sat on the floor playing with a set of dark gray, greasy building blocks, and my mother always cranked a sewing machine. Besides the noise of the sewing machine, the only other sound that could be heard was the ticking of an old table clock. Every once in a while, I would stop playing and stare blankly at the clock, waiting for it to strike. I never asked why the clock struck, and what the striking sound meant. I only remembered the clock's look and the Roman numerals on its face. I also remember the concrete floor was waxed and mopped, until not a speck of dust remained. I always sat on it and never felt cold. The scene stays in my memory like paint stained on clothes, or sand ingrained in flesh. Perhaps only my death can take it from me. I never thought of leaving the house, but it was inevitable."

"Sometimes, Mother would motion for me to come to her. With one hand spinning the sewing machine, and the other hand unbuttoning her clothes, she made me suck her milk. I was quite big then and could reach her breasts when I stood on the floor. To this day I can still feel it in my mouth, that soft and drooping thing, but I've forgotten the taste of her milk. I haven't drunk milk or eaten any dairy products since then. My mother always concentrated on sewing before, after, and during the time she fed me. She treated me with indifference. Of course, I had a father too, but he treated me with even more indifference. That was how my childhood went."

10

The other thing that Ah-Lan confessed was this, "By the time I walked out of that house, I'd reached middle school age.

"On the way to school, I often stopped before the bulletin board. There were all kinds of convicted criminals in the bulletins, and the word "rape" stirred fear deep in my heart. I knew it meant a man violated a woman. It was the most unimaginable thing in the world. There was another word called "adultery," which I associated with the obscene pictures on the walls of the public toilet—a man and a woman were together, and people would find out about them soon. I never had a sense of shame about things like that, only fear. If I can explain this to you, the rest will be easy to understand.

"There was a girl in our class, whose family didn't have other people to do it so the police station or the neighborhood committee often sent a policeman or an old woman to escort her to school. She would sit in a segregated seat in front of the whole class. She was given the nickname Public Bus, which meant whoever wanted could get on."

She was very pretty, and her body developed early, too. She wore a white undershirt and black cloth shoes. In the class, Ah-Lan would stare at her for long periods of time.

After class, boys and girls were divided into two groups, Public Bus was left in the middle.

"Whenever I saw her, I would think of those terrible words: rape, adultery. It is more accurate to say it was those words making me panic than to say her curves made my heart race. Every night before I fell asleep, my erection would last for a long time, as long as my panic.

"Public Bus told me she didn't do it with anyone. She just didn't like to go to school. That is, she was completely innocent of that terrible sin. But no one wanted to believe her. On the other hand, she admitted she had contacts with men from society, which meant she admitted to hanging around with hooligans. Therefore, she was escorted to the stage to accept denouncement.

"I still remember to this day how she looked standing with the other hooligan students on the stage. It was a strange time, sometimes students denounced their teachers, and sometimes teachers denounced their students. No matter who denounced whom, the ones who were escorted to the stage were all hooligans.

"I often saw this scene in my dreams: not she, but I, had small breasts and delicate shoulders and was escorted to the stage to be denounced, and my heart swelled with joy.

"In my dreams, Public Bus and I had merged into a single body."

11

That night, Ah-Lan confessed these things about himself. Of course, Xiao Shi didn't hear a single sentence because Ah-Lan hadn't spoken out loud at all, only confessing in his heart, or Xiao Shi heard but didn't take it in. At any rate, Xiao Shi wasn't a homosexual back then, all he wanted was to be shocked by tawdriness. Because of this, the two of them had different recollections of that night. To be truthful, Xiao Shi knew all the details of homosexual behavior—how they fooled around in public toilets, had anal and oral sex, and so on. He had heard enough stories of this sort. He just wanted to know how Ah-Lan took "two rods" at the same time, and how he managed to have an electric charge in both hands. But Ah-Lan said all this was made up out of nothing, or were stories about other people that came to be about him when they got passed around. Xiao Shi wasn't too happy about that, insisting that he tell something. Ah-Lan then spoke without enthusiasm about his first homosexual experience: it was with a high school classmate with the last name of Ma. The story would bore a non-homosexual; it happened at Ma's house—first they used their hands, and then their mouths. Ah-Lan tasted the flavor of that boy—he was salty. The incident made him understand the true meaning of sex, which was seeing a beautiful naked man moaning happily, with his face flushed and blue veins bulging. Meanwhile he tasted the primordial taste of life. At the time he thought he was so meek, so understanding that his heart burst with happiness. These words disgusted Xiao Shi, who felt Ah-Lan was very easy, and even wanted to beat him up immediately.

Looking back on the incident after so long gave Xiao Shi a new perspective. He had wanted to listen to Ah-Lan's "stories," anticipating them eagerly. But afterward he thought Ah-Lan was very easy. We might be tempted to say he detested Ah Lan's past pleasures, but put more accurately, he detested those pleasures because they had nothing to do with him. That is, either he had carried the seed of homosexuality for a long time, or he had always been gay and didn't realize it. Otherwise he wouldn't have listened to homosexual stories every time he worked the night shift.

12

A long time has passed, and as Xiao Shi sits under the desk lamp holding Ah-Lan's book in his hand, he finally figures out why back then Ah-Lan didn't want to talk about his homosexual experiences and gay lovers, but instead talked about irrelevant things. The answer to the riddle is: Ah-Lan loved him. And he asked Ah-Lan to talk about these things because he didn't love him then. He finally opens Ah-Lan's book.

The first story in Ah-Lan's book goes like this: Sometime in the ancient past, there was an army officer, or a palace guard—it doesn't matter which, the important thing was that he stood nine-feet tall with a purple beard and double pupils. His height and appearance actually don't matter either. The important thing was when he patrolled the tall palace walls, he caught a female thief and locked a chain around her neck. The woman had sloping shoulders and broad hips, as beautiful as a dragon princess. He could have sent her to prison, let her suffer prison life to the fullest, and then executed her; or he could have unlocked the chain and set her free. In the first instance, he would be turning her in to the authorities; in the second, he would be returning her to herself. There was actually a third choice: he could haul her away by the iron chain. That is, he could keep her for himself. In fact, that was what the female thief expected.

Ah-Lan wrote in his book: It was March, a warm spring, when the tender willows looked like mist, that the palace guard took her to the willow woods, pushed her down onto a filthy, black mound of remaining snow, and raped her. Afterward, she wrapped herself with her stained white robe and went back home with him. Ah-Lan said the coldness of the iron chain and the stain of the remnant of snow were components of the sensation of being raped cruelly. She felt such a feeling was wonderful. Xiao Shi thought of the whole story and believed that Ah-Lan was really sick. Three things, Ah-Lan's book, the stories Ah-Lan told him that night, and Ah-Lan's love, jumbled together as in a kaleidoscope. But three things became very clear to Ah-Lan. That is, before Ah-Lan wrote down this paragraph, he thought about himself sitting in the police station that night, looking at Xiao Shi's ferocious face, sensing his contempt for him. These feelings turned into the scene where the female thief was ravaged. She wore her snow-white robe and lay on a mound of remnant snow. This female thief was Ah-Lan. However, if you discount Ah-Lan's love for Xiao Shi, the scene remains obscure.

13

Ah-Lan said he thought about some of the things that he couldn't write in his book. He sat on the mattress savoring his own book. But the book wasn't complete—a book can't be wholly imaginary, and the imagination can't fit into a whole book, either. Actually, Ah-Lan's imagination also included the guard's sexual organ, hard as iron, cruel as iron, and cold as iron, too, piercing his (her) body. Torture and sex at the same time. But this part of his imagination was lost to his book. Ah-Lan thought perhaps he should write another book, revealing these feelings more openly.

Ah-Lan said the book, of course, was born of his love for Xiao Shi, or you could even say it was born of that long night that he and Xiao Shi spent in the police station. Even though much of it had been lost, it still retained its original shape. Whenever he thought of the book, he could gather that entire night in an embrace. And while he embraced that night, he would get an erection hard as iron. Ah-Lan lifted his terrycloth blanket, looked at that thing, and then covered it again. The thing was like a barometer of love. Ah-Lan didn't feel having the thing was necessary for him, because he was so submissive, offering himself up for insult, for torment, while the organ had bared fangs and unsheathed claws, completely out of character for him.

As Ah-Lan's middle school year was about to end, Public Bus was arrested and sent to a labor camp. He saw the scene from far away at the time. She held a bag that contained a basin and other stuff, walked up to the policemen, put down her things, and then offered her wrists one after the other to a set of handcuffs. It looked like an exchange at the market. Then she raised her handcuffed hands, gathered her hair, picked up her stuff, and left with them. The scene made Ah-Lan very envious—everything that happened beneath the quiet surface made Ah-Lan feel as though he had experienced it himself, and his heart swelled with joy.

14

In Ah-Lan's book, there was the following paragraph: The palace guard bound the female thief's neck and two hands in a chain and pulled her along like this, leaving the bustling town far behind, until he reached a riverbank. It was the end of winter and the beginning of spring, so the river was a stretch of bare riverbed, willow trees with new yellow branches lined the bank, and under the bank in the shade were patches of snow and ice. This scene heightened the cold of the iron chains for the female thief. She didn't know where the guard was taking her and had no choice but to follow.

The real situation was very different: Public Bus walked to the school's entrance in a group of people, with many students surrounding them. So they walked along in a crowd, as she carried her own things in two hands; the things seemed very heavy, so she struggled to walk with the bag—besides walking, she couldn't concentrate on anything else. Afterward, when she got into the police car, she finally had a chance to look around and saw Ah-Lan in the crowd. Seeing him, she gave him a smile, and wiggled several fingers as a farewell.

Ah-Lan said he believed it was Public Bus's beauty, gentleness, and submissiveness that got her arrested. Therefore, in his heart, being arrested became the synonym for beauty, gentleness, and submissiveness. Of course, Xiao Shi arrested him not because he had such characteristics, but because he'd heard his hands were electrically charged and his body could accommodate two rods, and so on. But Ah-Lan wanted to see things another way. That is, he wanted to believe Xiao Shi arrested him because of his beauty, gentleness, and submissiveness, despite knowing he might not be right.

15

Ah-Lan said Public Bus had had a long-standing premonition that she would be arrested. She told Ah-Lan, I've become very easy now. I'll get arrested eventually. Later Ah-Lan felt he was very easy, too, just after he graduated from high school.

Ah-Lan went to work on a farm (whether a farm or not, or some other job, it wasn't in the city anyway). He was a sad, unsociable person, but this temperament happened to take the leaders' fancy. The leaders thought he was an honest man and made him the mess officer in charge of the kitchen, so he got to go to the granary to buy rice regularly. After a while, he met a mess officer from the neighboring team, who also seemed sad and unsociable. Ah-Lan struck up a conversation with him and, in his naïveté, fell in love with him. The story unfolded very quickly. Not long after, on a festival night, Ah-Lan made love to the mess officer in a room in the neighboring team. In the middle of their lovemaking, or more accurately, after Ah-Lan finished doing his part for the other man and before the other man began doing his part for Ah-Lan, a gang of people suddenly jumped out, beat the hell out of Ah-Lan, took his money, and kicked him out of there. And then he walked the country road all night, counting the whitewashed trees on the roadside, which stood out in the dark. Like any young man who got a raw deal, he wanted revenge. But in fact revenge was impossible. For anyone to stand up for him that person would have had to admit he was a gay. At daybreak, entering the town, he could read in other people's eyes (Ah-Lan was in pretty bad shape then) how easy he had become. He even believed he was the easiest person in the world. From that moment on, he identified with Public Bus.

16

Ah-Lan said when he first came to the park, every evening, at the moment that colored lights went on, he would sense the presence of many tall, slender women promenading under the lights in black evening gowns that trailed along the floor. He felt he should be one of them. By midnight, he began to long for contact with flesh, as if it would have been too late if he were denied it now. Night's curtain fell, and the colorful lights came on, which made him feel urgent, eager to be loved by others. Xiao Shi knitted his eyebrows and said, Why talk all this nonsense? You'd better say something about yourself. Ah-Lan then smiled at this because it was actually a request for him to confess his love. If a love had no reason at all, it would be punished; otherwise it might be forgiven. This was the police station's logic. But the park was different; all the love there had no justification, but could always be forgiven, and therefore couldn't be called love. This was exactly why Ah-Lan despaired. He began to talk about these things: for example, how he would follow someone in the park, and after tailing him for a long time, they would go to a construction site or the top of a skyscraper to make love, or they would jerk each other off under the water in the public bathhouse. He said he didn't really like this sort of thing, because when people did this, they turned themselves into taps that sperm flowed out of. However, Xiao Shi believed Ah-Lan liked these things, otherwise why did he speak about them? As a policeman, he thought people wouldn't tell him something voluntarily; if they volunteered something, then they must have a particular reason. In short, he said with a grim expression, You had better get serious, you son of a bitch! He followed with a question, Do you think I'm a tap also? Ah-Lan avoided the question just by saying, Love should be punished. Without any punishment, it can't be called love.

17

Xiao Shi commented to Ah-Lan: You're just an easy son of a bitch. To his surprise, Ah-Lan took even such a judgment calmly. He said a girl once told him this: Some people are born easy. That girl was Public Bus. She and Ah-Lan sat at a small round table in Public Bus's home, cracking melon seeds. She said, Someone like me is born to seem the easiest around. This might be because she never performed any of the acts associated with someone who was damaged goods yet was called "damaged goods," and she was escorted to the stage for denouncement even though she never did any bad things, and so on. After a while, she said, Take a look at how easy I am. Then she took off all her clothes, sat down, lowered her head, and continued to crack melon seeds. Her hair slipped into her mouth, and she tossed her head back and got it out. Then she noticed that Ah-Lan wasn't looking at her body, so she said, You can look at me. It doesn't matter. So Ah-Lan raised his head and looked at her, his face blushing. But she was as calm as ever. She spat out a melon seed shell and said, Touch me. Ah-Lan reached out his trembling hand and chose her breasts. When his fingertips touched her skin, Ah-Lan shuddered as if shocked by electricity. But she didn't seem to feel anything. Then she laid her arms across the table, let her hair down over her shoulders, hiding her body and Ah-Lan's caressing hand under the table, and said calmly, What do you think? Suddenly, she saw a fly, grabbed the nearby swatter and stood up to kill it. At that moment Public Bus didn't seem easy at all, not like her usual self. Because she had a slender and pale body, the bulge of her breasts, and belly also, seemed interesting. Only when she wore clothes and covered herself did she appear easy.

Public Bus told Ah-Lan everyone was born easy, which could never be changed. The more you want to disguise your easiness, the easier you'll be. The only way to escape was to admit your own easiness, and try to enjoy it. When Ah-Lan was a little boy and sat on the concrete floor playing with building blocks, he would often unconsciously fondle his penis. Then his mother would pounce on him, saying he was behaving like a hooligan, threatening to cut it off, and so on. Then she would say she was going to call Uncle Policeman, who would take him away and lock him in prison. When the scolding failed, she tied him up and forced him to sit on the concrete floor with his hands tied behind him. When Ah-Lan sat this way with his hands behind him, he felt he was getting an erection and became unusually excited. All the time he waited for Uncle Policeman to come, to take him to prison. From then on, an Uncle Policeman with a peaked cap and handcuffs hanging from his belt became his true dream lover. Now, such an Uncle Policeman was sitting in front of him; however, Xiao Shi was ten years younger than Ah-Lan. It was from this position that he admitted he was easy.

When Ah-Lan thought about how Public Bus exposed her naked body to him, how smooth her satinlike skin was, he wanted to say all this should also belong to Xiao Shi. He wanted to dedicate everything he had to Xiao Shi—but he didn't say so. Firstly, Public Bus no longer had her seventeen-year-old body; secondly, this kind of devotion was too shocking and frightening. So the idea dispersed from his mind like a puff of dark blue smoke.

When he'd just returned from the farm, Ah-Lan said, he wanted to give up his homosexuality, that is, to not be so easy. So he went to the hospital. There a doctor in a white smock sat at a desk plucking his nasal hair. He gave Ah-Lan two stacks of pictures; one was of males, the other was of females; he also gave him two glasses of white liquid, one was milk, the other emetic. Then he told Ah-Lan to drink a mouthful of milk when he looked at the women's pictures and a mouthful of emetic when he looked at the men's pictures, and then he left. Ah-Lan began to throw up. The surroundings and what he was doing made him feel even easier than before.

Ah-Lan skimmed through the whole set of pictures, whose cheap manufacture and vulgar figures disgusted him. He didn't especially dislike women, nor did he especially like men. He just hated ugly things and liked beautiful things. After a while, Ah-Lan put down the pictures, sat by the sink and drank the glass of emetic one mouthful after another. When he was vomiting, he tried his best to remain graceful (looking at himself in the mirror above the sink). He even began to enjoy vomiting.

Xiao Shi told Ah-Lan, I have never come across someone like you before—that is, no one would admit he's easy. Therefore, this is true easiness. When he poured forth his high talk, he didn't notice the radiance of Ah-Lan's face, or that he was making a pass at him. That is, Xiao Shi didn't notice that Ah-Lan loved him. He only paid attention to the obvious, that there were a policeman and a criminal in the room, a good person and an easy person; that there was one who was admonishing and one who was being admonished. He didn't notice what was beneath.

18

When Ah-Lan sat in the police station, he felt he was the woman in the white robe, tied into a five-petal position, lifted onto an oxcart, and carried off into the mist. In this desperate situation, on the cart, she fell in love with the executioner. The executioner looked solemn, dignified, and expressionless (like a fool), so the fact that Ah-Lan fell in love with him originally was not without ulterior motive. In this story, under a white robe, all the slyness, evil, and lust were banished, what was left was only innocence, delicacy, and tenderness. Under the white robe, she was experiencing herself and anticipating the sharpness of the knife-edge on her neck.

Ah-Lan talked about his feelings; he often felt wronged for no reason, wanted to give himself, to give himself to someone. At those times he and his imaginary female thief in her white robe merged into one. The oxcart jolted along the slope and stopped in the meadow. She and the executioner got off the cart, strolled into the meadow, as if they were taking a walk. But it was to be the last walk of her life. And the executioner held her leather-bound wrists, like a shadow following its body, and the feeling was wonderful. She was held tightly, and that was also a wonderful feeling. She was held tightly like this until they reached a dirt pit on a slope. The pit was very shallow, but she wouldn't have liked a deep pit either. Then she threw herself into the executioner's arms and gave herself away at that moment. But Ah-Lan didn't write this feeling into his book. A book can't contain everything.

Later, the love story that Ah-Lan told went like this: Several years before, he was still very young, very handsome, and at the time had won quite a reputation in his circle. One day, when he walked in the street with a few friends, or a few admirers, a boy watched him from far away. Timid, he was afraid to come over to strike up a conversation with him. Later, they did manage to make each other's acquaintance. The boy was a grade school teacher from the countryside. He had only heard of someone called Ah-Lan in the city, fell in love with him, then walked up to him and said, I love you. He also said, You can do whatever you want to do with me. It was a desperate love, and also a desperate devotion, and you couldn't refuse it. But this despair was easier to understand than Ah-Lan's, because it came out of poverty. Ah-Lan had been to his home and saw the yellow-mud hut full of cracks, a wooden bed propped up on four glass bottles, and a wretched old couple stupefied by poverty and hard work. In that shabby house, Ah-Lan fell in love with the grade school teacher, feeling like an elegant and richly arrayed noblewoman, and on that wooden bed, he asked the schoolteacher to use him. He thought the feeling was wonderful.

Ah-Lan also wanted to say the boy was so poor that his house had nothing but four bare walls, yet he wore trendy jeans and drove an expensive racing motorcycle. Like all country people, he was anxious to keep up appearances. He walked up to Ah-Lan and said, I love you, and I belong to you alone. He showed Ah-Lan not only his beautiful exterior, but also his shabby house, and his embarrassment when he had no one to turn to—that is, he offered every hint to show Ah-Lan the way to love him. But Ah-Lan's decision went far beyond his expectations; he was going to love him the way a millionaire was loved, or an emperor. So what Ah-Lan wanted to say was this: how wonderful it was to be born beautiful—all kinds of exceptions will be made for him in the world, as if he were a god.

Perhaps Ah-Lan told other stories about himself and the boy, such as how they set a net to catch birds by the riverside, but what they caught were some worthless sparrows. Or, how they transported clothes for sale over a long distance, but ended up losing money. These stories all concluded in the same way: Ah-Lan spread out his body in that shabby mud hut, asking the boy to love him and vent his despair. The house was always lit with a bare bulb, and on the crack-covered walls, several big, fierce-looking cockroaches were always crawling around. At midnight, fog floated into the room, and by the bedside old books and newspapers piled up—poor people hated throwing even a piece of paper away—to be loved by someone in despair is best. But Xiao Shi didn't understand the story at all. He said, Look at what crap you talk, you son of a bitch. Is that called love? Ah-Lan had no choice but to finish the story hastily. Later the grade school teacher wanted Ah-Lan to marry his sister, so the three of them could live together. The suggestion disgusted Ah-Lan and he refused. He could love him, but didn't want to be dragged into that kind of life. Now there wouldn't be anyone to look at him timidly, or come over to tell him in despair: I love you. Sometimes, being young, pretty, and sexy also gave you hope. But Ah-Lan isn't these things anymore.

Ah-Lan still looks all right now. But he had begun to use makeup; he plucked his eyebrows and coated his face with a layer of cold cream. The thing that concerned him most was that his skin had dimmed, and the skin over his joints had begun to wrinkle. He wanted to maintain a beautiful young man's tall, slender, and gleaming body. Xiao Shi believed he was perverse, but Ah-Lan didn't think so himself. That sort of body is called beautiful, whether it belongs to a man or a woman.

19

That night, in the police station, Ah-Lan also talked about a transvestite in the park. The man wore a black skirt and a pair of sunglasses and looked like a woman. If you missed the blue veins on the back of his hands, you wouldn't think he was a man. The man walked back and forth in the park, talking to no one. Maybe he just wanted to display himself. Most people probably wouldn't have noticed he was a man, but homosexuals knew immediately. Ah-Lan sympathized with him very much, and tried to strike up a conversation with him, but he refused. This was because he refused to admit that he was a man, even a gay man. It made Ah-Lan realize his despair was even deeper than his own.

The young policeman also knew about the man. He pulled out his drawer, which contained his whole set of tools for committing his crime. The incident happened this way: he'd made curves for his male body by winding strips of cloth; however, he also would have to go to the toilet. One day, when he unwound the strips of cloth in a women's toilet, a lady saw him. As you can imagine, the latter let out a scream and the guy was arrested. In the police station, Xiao Shi volunteered to unwind his cloth strips and told him jubilantly, You have prickly heat, you son of a bitch. That was how they confiscated the guy's headgear, dresses, and a large quantity of sweat-drenched ribbon gauze, enough to wrap up quite a few mummies. Speaking about this to Ah-Lan still put Xiao Shi into high spirits, which made Ah-Lan feel a little sad. He'd been outside the police station that day and saw this guy in ragged clothes leaving in embarrassment. From his mascaraed eyes came two black teardrops. The incident had its reasonable aspect, because that man was so easy, so desperate, he deserved to be shamed; but it also had its cruel aspect, because the shaming was so sordid, so vulgar. Even a murderer would receive a Judgment Pronouncement Rally, a pre-execution ritual. Shame and ridicule were not the same. That is, even a low and easy person also wants respect.

Needless to say, Xiao Shi was shocked to hear these words. He had never thought that a low and easy person also wants respect, so he didn't know whether to laugh or cry. Because he heard so many things that he had never heard before, he felt Ah-Lan was a learned person, even though his learning was a dirty kind. He wanted to offer Ah-Lan respect, too, so he formally renewed his acquaintance with Ah-Lan, having them make mutual introductions to each other, and even addressing Ah-Lan as a teacher. His doing so was not without teasing, but Ah-Lan accepted it. This was because being called "teacher" suited the atmosphere of humiliation and torment.

20

In the book, Ah-Lan wrote: The guard led the white-robed female thief to his house and chained her to the pillar in the middle of the room. In doing so he committed the major crime of embezzlement. Beautiful woman criminals were public property there and had to be humiliated and tortured to death in broad daylight. His taking her home, therefore, constituted embezzlement.

What actually happened that night was: a rainstorm descended after midnight, and the air became cool and fresh, which made Xiao Shi feel sleepy. He yawned and said, You can take a nap. He himself planned to sleep on his office desk, and Ah-Lan could lean in a chair against the wall. He hesitated over one thing for a while, and then finally made up his mind; he took out a pair of handcuffs and said, Teacher Ah-Lan, I'm sorry, but it's the rule. He didn't just say so but was truly embarrassed. However, Ah-Lan calmly held out his right hand. When Ah-Lan gave him his left hand, Xiao Shi said, Not like that. You have to turn around. He handcuffed Ah-Lan behind his back and helped him sit down. When he handcuffed Ah-Lan, he felt guilty, so he wanted to show some gentleness, more or less—asking him if he were hot or not, and loosening his collar. Then he went back to his desk and sat down. He saw Ah-Lan's face flushed with anticipation, showing no sign of sleepiness. This made it impossible for him to go to sleep.

21

When Xiao Shi met Ah-Lan's eyes, he felt very embarrassed, because he seldom faced someone alone who was handcuffed by him—he was only a naughty and inexperienced boy. He even called this person "teacher," a person who had admitted he was easy, which embarrassed him all the more. He felt it wasn't proper to handcuff him, but couldn't open them either—if he removed Ah-Lan's handcuffs, it meant he was aware and afraid of Ah-Lan's masochistic tendencies—under the circumstances, playing dumb was best.

Ah-Lan spoke of one of his romances. The person seldom came to the park. When he came, he would wear a windbreaker and sunglasses and stand at a corner of the park . . . he was a painter who lived in an apartment by himself. His home was furnished simply, so it appeared spacious. One of the things he liked to do was to bring out a low coffee table, spread a piece of batiked cloth (or a piece of plain white cloth) on it, set out one or two pieces of porcelain plates or vases, and arrange flowers or fruits on them; then he would tie Ah-Lan's hands behind his back with rawhide and bend him over the coffee table, either to do him or to paint his body. In the second case, he would take pictures of Ah-Lan from behind. Most of the time he painted him first and then did him. Ah-Lan felt the click of the shutter as cruel and piercingly cold, and gradually the difference between the camera and sexual organ blurred. He told Xiao Shi that now when he saw a black camera sometimes, he would get hot down there . . . he liked the black, lusterless, round shape of a camera, and also liked everything with that kind of shape. One day, Ah-Lan called at the painter's apartment, and the door didn't open for a long time, and then he caught a glimpse of a woman in the apartment. The painter said, You can come back in the evening. Of course, Ah-Lan never went back there again. But he didn't really hate him. He offered only one comment about the incident, "It's over." Later, when he saw the painter in the park, Ah-Lan only greeted him from a distance, or watched him from far away.

That is, he felt he had been used. This surprised Xiao Shi very much, and he kept asking him what he meant, and then he delivered his conclusion: You're really easy, you son of a bitch. This made Ah-Lan bow his head again. After a while he looked up and said, The word "jian" in English is "easy." That was what he was like, when you waved him over, he came, and when you waved him away, he went. He was happy at being so easy. This struck Xiao Shi dumb and he couldn't find the words to denounce him.

22

Xiao Shi carefully marks his place on the page with his little finger, gets a bookmark, and puts it between the pages. He closes the book and lets time stop there. What confuses him is that up to that point, he hadn't fallen in love with Ah-Lan and didn't see any sign that he might fall in love with him, and most of that night had passed.

Ah-Lan was known for being easy in his work unit. We've mentioned that he's a writer, which meant he used to work in a cultural center and sometimes wrote some small articles and so on. Because he came out as gay long ago, he accepted the following treatment long ago. He had to arrive at the cultural center very early, to mop the floor, get boiling water, and scrub and clean the toilet. By going along with this, he was trying to make a place for himself, or we might say he sought out the easiest place. But he couldn't make a place for himself, because "easiness" has no place.

Ah-Lan also said every time he went out, that is, every time he put on a four-pocketed gray uniform, and carried a leatherette case and went to the cultural center to work, or merged into the flood of bike traffic; or sat with eyes half-shut among people attending a meeting; he would feel he was just muddling along on his way to a dead end because he was trying to hide his easiness. Every time he went to work, he couldn't conceal his compulsions: to go to the painter's house, to be tied up, to be smeared, painted, and used. Only at those times did he feel his image of himself suited what he was doing, that is, fit his nature. He said, Because millions of people wear these clothes, attend these meetings, carry these cases, how could we not be easy?

23

For Ah-Lan, the most unfortunate thing was that he really loved Public Bus. Perhaps we should call him bisexual. Public Bus was his wife now, and they lived in Ah-Lan's childhood house. His current situation put him in a dilemma, because wanting to love and wanting to be love contradicted each other. Every day he would arrive home to her standing before him dressed nicely, greeting him very politely, Welcome home. Public Bus always wore clothes for going out at home: sheath skirt, short jacket, long silk stockings, and makeup. Even when she sat in a chair, she would keep her upper body straight, incomparably graceful. Ah-Lan would close in on her without provocation, grab her by the shoulders, and throw her down onto the bed. Then Public Bus would lower her voice and say: Can I shut the door? Ah-Lan would push her back down on the bed, unbutton her, loosen her bra, and push it up—until Public Bus looked like a fish with a sliced-open belly. When Ah-Lan caressed her and made love to her, she scratched at the wallpaper with her little finger and looked thoughtful. Not until they finished their business did she stop and ask Ah-Lan: Was it good? As if she were asking about something ordinary. She would look virginal then. Public Bus was always tender and quiet, but only with Ah-Lan.

When Ah-Lan withdrew from Public Bus's body, she was as messy as a junk stall. Looking back on how she appeared before lovemaking, anyone would believe that she had offered herself for humiliation and torment. She silently got to her feet, took off her wrinkled clothes, folded them, put on old, shabby clothing, carefully washed off her makeup, and went out to shop for groceries. Only when she was about to go out would she carefully remove her makeup and put on old, shabby clothes. When she dressed neatly and richly, she was waiting for sex; when she left her hair uncombed and her face unwashed, it meant she would reject sex. This was the complete opposite of other people. In this way, she was as eccentric as Madonna, who liked to wear her underwear on the outside.

24

That afternoon, when the young policeman arrested Ah-Lan, his wife got wind of it immediately because it was a small town.

Ah-Lan's wife (Public Bus) was shopping for groceries in the market when someone told her that Ah-Lan got picked up. She just said, "That serves him right!" Then she asked which place they took him. Generally speaking, picked up is picked up, but with gays, they could be sent to the palace or the harem,* and going to the palace wasn't too bad. The lady had the situation cleared up for her, didn't seem worried, and then went home and did household chores, trying to keep calm. She was still considered young, but appeared a little haggard; still pretty, but beginning to lose her looks. That was her appearance.

When evening came, Ah-Lan's wife cooked dinner and ate by herself, and even saved some for Ah-Lan; then she went out and called her girlfriend from the pay phone downstairs. Her first sentence was: That bastard Ah-Lan got taken in again. I believe her girlfriend didn't know why Ah-Lan got taken in, but knew Ah-Lan often got taken in, so she thought of him as an ordinary hooligan. Her girlfriend asked her what she was going to do about it, and she said if he didn't come back tonight, let him stay inside; if he didn't come back tomorrow, she was going to the police station to pick him up—what else could she do? As we know, if a homosexual is detained and his wife comes to pick him up, the policemen are happy to hand him over. This is because they believe he will suffer more at his wife's hands. Everything the police do follows the principle of increasing suffering. Her girlfriend didn't want to hear this. Through the telephone we could hear her persuading Ah-Lan's wife to dump him, "Why so faithful to one man?" But Ah-Lan's wife didn't want to discuss practical matters; she just wept and said she was fed up with it. After that, she dried her tears and said, Sorry to bother you. Then she hung up and went back home. Ah-Lan didn't observe this, but could imagine it all.

25

Ah-Lan had written in his book: The guard locked the female thief in a pale blue house, made of stone; the inside walls were painted snow-white and straw covered the floor near them. It had the feel of a stable, a fitting habitation for people who were

---

* *Palace* is homosexual slang for the police station; *harem* is slang for the detention camp, where treatment could be much more severe than at the police station.

easy by nature. He brought her to the wall, made her sit down, locked the chain around her neck into the iron hoop on the wall, and then brought out a set of wooden stocks. Seeing the shocked and frightened expression of the female thief, he bent down in front of her feet and said, because her feet were beautiful, he had to nail the stocks shut. So the female thief put her ankles into the semicircular grooves in the wood and let the guard close the other half and nail them in. She felt unusually happy as she watched the guard doing this.

After a while, the guard brought out another set of wooden stocks and told her that her neck and hands were also beautiful and he had to nail them down, too. So another set of wooden stocks was added to the female thief's neck. Then the guard took the iron chain from her neck and went out, locking the wooden gate with the chain. After he left, the female thief looked around the stone house for a long time—she stood up, moved around the room like a spread pencil compass. When she reached the doorway, she saw a pink room outside.

In the evening, Ah-Lan's wife stayed home alone and went to bed early. She tossed in bed and couldn't fall asleep. Then she made love to herself. After she finished she began to sob, which shows that she still loved Ah-Lan, and couldn't remain indifferent to what he did. But in Ah-Lan's book, there wasn't anything that referred to Ah-Lan's wife. He didn't want Public Bus to know that he loved her.

At midnight, a heavy rain fell. Public Bus got up to shut the window. She wore white knit underwear, and the house was pale blue. The house that Ah-Lan lived in later was also this color. She shut the window and lay back down to sleep. When Public Bus fell asleep, she placed her hands on her chest as if she were dead.

When it rained that night, Xiao Shi's wife Dian Zi was fast sleep. Their house was pink. The lighted desk lamp had a pink shade. Dian Zi wore red underwear and made fang-and-claw gestures toward the empty side of Xiao Shi's double bed.

26

Xiao Shi admitted that when he saw how arrogantly the pretty misses in the state-run shops or joint-venture restaurants treated their countrymen, he wanted to arrest them and force them to squat by the walls of the police station. He also said every now and then there would be some wild chick (sex worker was another name for them) squatting by the walls. These girls found it especially difficult to squat, because they often wore such tight skirts. They would have had no choice then, but to put their thighs together and press their hands on their thighs, so they could seem graceful. He thought they looked even prettier this way than sitting up straight. When they were handcuffed and escorted away, they would let down their hair to cover half of their faces. This also made them more attractive than those girls who parted their hair and kept their faces blank. So, in Xiao Shi's mind, sex objects looked prettiest and sexiest when they offered themselves up for humiliation and torment. Therefore, he had something in common with Ah-Lan. But there was a difference between them, too: he was on the side that gave humiliation, and Ah-Lan was on the side that received humiliation; he belonged with the tormenters, and Ah-Lan belonged with the tormented. Figuring this out embarrassed Xiao Shi—it was time to draw a line between them.

27

Xiao Shi looked out of the window, and the eastern sky began to show a little bit of white. This relaxed him, and he stretched himself and said, Thank God, the night's finally over. He also said that he had never felt so tired before on his night shifts. But Ah-Lan had a sense of urgency. Xiao Shi yawned over and over, took the keys, walked up to Ah-Lan, and said, Turn around. I'm off duty now. When Ah-Lan hesitated, Xiao Shi said, If you like to wear these things, go buy a set for yourself. This one is public property. Ah-Lan turned around and Xiao Shi lazily opened his handcuffs, and then Ah-Lan whispered to him: I love you. This left Xiao Shi dazed for a while. Either he heard but couldn't believe it, or he thought he hadn't heard clearly. Whatever the case, he didn't want to inquire further. He straightened up and said: I think it would have been better to keep you handcuffed. Then he walked away. The blush on his face, though, he couldn't hide anymore.

28

Ah-Lan told Xiao Shi that he was gentle, submissive, and understanding. He felt in his heart that he was a woman, and even more than that. When he appeared in front of a handsome and sexy man, he would feel tender and soft as water, a spring of clear, cool water that suddenly materialized in front of you after you had trudged a long way. He could appear very beautiful, because women didn't have a monopoly on beauty. He mentioned especially the times the painter placed him over the low table in that room full of mirrors. He saw the lower half of his behind in the mirror: taut legs, small hips, and a part of his scrotum between his legs. He believed it was a big mistake to say that only women were beautiful. The most beautiful thing was to live in the world and offer yourself up for humiliation and torment.

In Ah-Lan's book, there was this paragraph: The female thief knelt in that pink room, bending and stretching to scrub the floor. The long stocks on her neck had been removed, and she wore hand shackles, and her feet were widely splayed and nailed into wooden stocks. In front of her stood a wooden bucket of water, and in her hands was a scrub brush. She arched and stretched out her body, like a looper caterpillar. The guard sat to the side watching; after a while, he stood up, approached the rear of the female thief, lifted her white robe, and went at her from behind . . . meanwhile she continued to scrub the floor.

When Ah-Lan talked about these things, he was very feminine, very gentle and charming, which made Xiao Shi's flesh crawl. However, when Ah-Lan spoke, his hands were locked behind his back, and his legs crossed, like a fine lady, which also looked a little seductive to Xiao Shi. So he knitted his eyebrows and asked, Are you a man or a woman after all, you son of a bitch? Ah-Lan said, It's not important. When you want to give love, you're a man; when you want to receive love, you're a woman. There is nothing more unimportant than whether you're a man or woman.

29

Ah-Lan gave as an example the love between him and that unknown grade school teacher. As I mentioned earlier, that night, in the yellowish mud hut in the countryside, after the grade school teacher said, You can do whatever you want with me, Ah-Lan kissed him passionately, asked him to lie flat on the bed, kissed his chest, the inside of his elbow, his chin, and caressed him, calming him down, and without his noticing returned the initiative of the lovemaking to him. He said, That night, he wanted to give love at the beginning, but all of a sudden, he felt tender and soft as water, so he switched to receiving. You can love, you can also be loved, and these are the most beautiful things in the world.

30

In Ah-Lan's story, after the female thief scrubbed the floor, she took out a small basket full of fragrant herbs. She continued to arch and stretch like a looper caterpillar, taking care to sprinkle the herbs evenly. She concentrated on this, as if she cared about nothing else. Meanwhile, the guard sat there monitoring her. Ah-Lan thought to himself that this kind of monitoring was very important. Without the monitoring, all the hard work would have had no meaning at all.

However, what Ah-Lan recalled (he sat on the mattress now) was very different from what Xiao Shi was thinking. That night, after he told Xiao Shi that he could give love, and could also receive love, he tenderly lowered his head and said, I love you. That is, he was ready to receive humiliation and torment from Xiao Shi. So Xiao Shi dragged him outside, put him under the tap, and drenched him; and then he dragged him back, put him in the chair, and gave him a flurry of slaps. All the while Ah-Lan was handcuffed from behind, feeling inexplicable joy. After all this happened, Xiao Shi's face suddenly froze in panic. Ah-Lan took the chance to kiss his palm saying, Beauty is something that comes when you beckon it. Then Xiao Shi opened his handcuffs. Ah-Lan showed Xiao Shi a picture of himself made-up as a woman. You couldn't tell in the picture that the woman was Ah-Lan. On the surface, it was only a picture of a naked woman, but knowing what was beneath the surface lent it a perverse beauty. Ah-Lan conquered Xiao Shi in this way—because of this, Ah-Lan felt that night was especially precious.

In Ah-Lan's book, the female thief did everything that she was supposed to do and then returned to the doorway of her own room. Perhaps it should be called the doorway of her prison cell. She knelt on the floor, offered her handcuffed hands to the guard, waiting for her wooden handcuffs to be removed and replaced with the long stocks. She concentrated on this with all her heart, as if nothing were more important.

31

Ah-Lan wrote in his book: sometimes the guard would remove the stocks from the female thief, lead her out of the pale blue room and into the pink one, chain her to a dressing table, and leave. Then the female thief would put makeup on, carefully painting her eyebrows and eyes to make herself more beautiful—that is, to make herself look even easier.

At the police station, Ah-Lan told the young policeman that in the painter's apartment, he had dressed up as a woman many times, a nude model either to be rendered as an oil painting, or to be photographed. He said, As long as you yearn to be loved, beauty will come when you beckon. For him, being a model meant being loved. Besides, every time the painter finished his painting, he would make love to Ah-Lan. The painter said if he didn't make love, his work would be incomplete. For the painter, love was a kind of art; but for Ah-Lan, art was a kind of love. Xiao Shi remembered those words. He stroked Ah-Lan's book and believed the book was love. He took out a picture and placed it in the book, and the picture was of Ah-Lan in women's clothes.

Later, the young policeman pulled out the drawer and left the room. The drawer contained the whole set of the transvestite's costume—jacket, skirt, cloth strips to wind around his body, headgear, and makeup. Ah-Lan sat at the desk and began to dress himself as a woman. He painted his face as if he were painting a picture. This was art, and in his words, art was a kind of love, and love meant offering yourself up for humiliation, for torment. The young policeman returned to the police station, and through the glass in the door, saw an incomparably beautiful woman sitting at his desk. He was stunned by such beauty and didn't push the door to enter for a long time.

32

The woman that Ah-Lan dressed up as wore a black dress, which happened to be Ah-Lan's favorite color. When the young policeman finally entered the office, Ah-Lan stood up, and walked over to him with grace, casting his eyes around the room charmingly. He bent slightly to gather up his skirt and then calmly knelt. He unzipped the young policeman's pants while he moistened his lips with his tongue . . . the scene that Xiao Shi bowed to see was incredible to him. He raised his arms midair, like a surgeon in an operating room . . . at last, he lowered his hands, pressed them on Ah-Lan's head. Meanwhile, he raised his head to the sky in ecstasy.

Sitting on the mattress now, Ah-Lan moistened his lips, lifted the blanket and put his hand underneath . . . he felt ecstasy, too. This was because Xiao Shi used to feel ecstasy and Ah-Lan remembered that with intense pleasure. Everything that happens in love offered itself to be savored in memory.

33

In the morning, the light reached the pale blue room first. The female thief sat on the straw, wearing long stocks on her neck and wooden stocks on her feet, as if nothing had happened during the night. But her hair was uncombed and her face had a residue of makeup.

In Ah-Lan's gray room, as the first rays of the morning appeared, Public Bus rose. She carefully applied her makeup, put on her best clothes, and then sat down at the table, resting her two hands on it and facing an alarm clock. She was waiting for time to pass so she could go to pick up Ah-Lan.

That morning, Ah-Lan's wife went to pick him up. Because it was so early, the whole city looked like a ghost town. In the street, she saw Ah-Lan walking toward her, with a weary expression and a face smudged with black. She stopped in the middle of the street when she saw him, waiting for him to come to her. When Ah-Lan got to her, she turned around and walked off with him, shoulder to shoulder. She didn't ask what happened that night. Then Ah-Lan gave her his hand, and she held his wrist—the way she held his penis in the evenings. Anything that could be held was a contract with reality, which would be broken as soon as you loosed your grip. Ah-Lan's wife never questioned him; she would only shed a few tears in private, and when she reappeared, she would be as tender and submissive as ever. But this didn't work on Ah-Lan at all. Ah-Lan was a man, but it didn't really matter; in his bones, he was the same as she. From a certain point of view, what happened between them was really homosexual.

That night, Ah-Lan had dressed up as a woman. One could see it from the traces of makeup on his face. But Public Bus didn't ask. When they went back home, she just poured some water from the thermos and let him wash the smudges off his face, and then she asked Ah-Lan if he wanted to eat something. Ah-Lan said he could eat a little. But he didn't just eat a little, he was very hungry. After that, Public Bus said, You can sleep for a while. I'm going to do some grocery shopping. But right then, Ah-Lan grabbed her hand, which was a signal. Public Bus couldn't help screaming, "What do you want? What do you want to do?" There was a bit of fear in her voice. Though Ah-Lan bowed his head, one could imagine his expression: embarrassed but also a little insensitive. In short, Ah-Lan behaved like a little bastard who would have slept with his own mother. Seeing this, Public Bus heaved a sigh and said, All right. She walked to the bed, faced the wall, and began to take off her clothes. Then she lay on the bed, covered her body with the quilt and her eyes with the back of her hand. Ah-Lan came over, lifted the quilt and began to screw her violently. We can explain this by saying that Ah-Lan didn't get release for himself that night; he only was a recipient of the release—referring just to body fluids, of course. As Ah-Lan thrust with the power of a galloping horse, Public Bus wept and said over and over, You don't love me. But by the time Ah-Lan finished, Public Bus had also finished her crying. She took out her handkerchief to dry her face, and assumed a calm expression. Then Ah-Lan lay back beside her and said, I do want to love you. As for whether or not Public Bus was satisfied, we don't know.

34

Light came into the pink room, and the guard remained fast asleep, naked with his body splayed out in an X . . . Dian Zi was also fast asleep. She slept differently from the guard—across the double bed on the diagonal with her face buried in the pillow.

Meanwhile, Xiao Shi walked over to the window and looked out. Before him lay the empty park, and Ah-Lan had long ago disappeared into the morning mist. He felt that Ah-Lan had given him back the right to choose. He could savor the memory of the night or not; he could beckon for Ah-Lan to come back, or he could refuse to do so. The meaning of the encounter lay in his understanding that he was a homosexual also.

35

When Xiao Shi was with Ah-Lan, he still felt Ah-Lan was very easy. He felt that even after they made love. They always did it in places like air-raid shelters, where they lit a candle and spread a ragged mat. After they finished, he would always add, consciously or unconsciously, You're really easy, you son of a bitch. But Ah-Lan never responded and would only say, Do you mind if I hug you? So Xiao Shi would turn over lazily to present Ah-Lan with his back, saying, condescendingly, So hug. The incident shows that Xiao Shi didn't love Ah-Lan back then, but only fell in love with him later.

Xiao Shi opened the book again. The story ended this way: One day, when the female thief woke up, she walked up to the wooden gate to look outside; there wasn't anyone in the pink room, even the iron chain that locked the gate had disappeared. She nudged the door with the end of the wooden stocks, and the door swung open. She walked into the pink room, slowly making her way around the silk screen. There was a bed behind the screen—no one was sleeping on the bed, which was just a rough wooden board. The furniture, leaning over or fallen, suggested the owner would never return. She slowly moved to the doorway, opened the door with the edge of the long stocks, and discovered with great surprise that the house was located in a garden. It was a warm spring in March, and the garden bloomed with luxuriant flowers.

Later, Ah-Lan left town and moved somewhere else. Xiao Shi went to the train station at the time to see him off. So, there was an embarrassing scene in the station; under the scrutiny of the two women, the two men felt very awkward. The young policeman blushed and called Public Bus, Sister-in-law, but Public Bus looked at him with ice-cold eyes. Only when she turned to Dian Zi did her eyes become warm. The two women paired up immediately, and Xiao Shi and Ah-Lan paired up, which made it look like two gay couples were talking. However, Xiao Shi and Ah-Lan were actually in the women's custody.

As the train was leaving, Xiao Shi felt an indescribable impulse; he began to feel love for Ah-Lan in his very bones. Despite the gaze of the two women, he couldn't help reaching out his hand and touching him. Obviously, doing such a thing at that moment was inappropriate. But the more forbidden something is, the more people want to do it, everyone has encountered this sort of thing—he fell in love right then. That is, not only did he admit he was gay, but he also admitted that he was just as easy as Ah-Lan.

36

Ah-Lan lives in a place of glittering lights and flowing wine now. If you looked down from his room, you would see a big street. He walks around the room with white cloth wound around his waist, like Gandhi. But the difference between this Gandhi and the real one lay in his lips, moist and bright, as if he used makeup. On the nightstand beside his bed, there was a frame with Xiao Shi's picture in it. To this day, he loves Xiao Shi just as Xiao Shi loves him. However, when he looks at this picture now, he would recall how rushed Xiao Shi always seemed, especially before their lovemaking. You had to say to him, Why don't you take off your jacket? Then he would remember to take off his jacket; you also had to say, Take off your watch, it scratches. And then he would take off his watch. At those moments Xiao Shi was cross-eyed, which maybe his wife had never seen. Now facing Xiao Shi's picture and recalling these things, he smiled an understanding smile. But not back then—because he was busy receiving Xiao Shi's love then. So Ah-Lan believed the most beautiful part about love was that you could savor the memory forever. When he savored the memory now, he didn't think he was easy.

In the evening, when Ah-Lan sat on the mattress, he heard footsteps outside, and then the turning of a key in the lock. He hurriedly hid Xiao Shi's picture, lay back on the mattress, and closed his eyes. Then Public Bus walked in. She kicked off her high heels and went into the bathroom. Then she emerged in a white nightgown and quietly lay beside Ah-Lan, stroking the coverlet between them with the back of her hand and her fingers, as if to draw an invisible line. She was still very tender and submissive, but no one knows whether or not she still loved Ah-Lan. Therefore, the house felt like an ancient tomb.

37

Later, the female thief returned to the place where the guard had caught her and laid all of her stocks and chains beneath the tall palace walls; she paced back and forth, watching every passerby. And the young policeman also paced back and forth in the park, sometimes he approached a group of homosexuals, but he didn't have the courage to strike up a conversation with them. Ah-Lan was still irreplaceable in his heart. In our society, homosexuals are like icebergs in the ocean who meet sometimes and part at other times, completely unable to act on their own. In this respect, Xiao Shi was an iceberg who had just started to float. As an iceberg, one should love the ocean currents and wind lightly, and during the occasional encounter, love another iceberg wholeheartedly. But Xiao Shi hadn't learned the way.

Xiao Shi closes Ah-Lan's book.

Xiao Shi began to sense his own easiness: he looked around the pitch-black room. In this room in the daytime, no one would talk to him face-to-face. Besides that, drinking glasses could best show how matters stood. There were plenty of porcelain cups in the police station, and originally people used these cups casually, but now the cup he used was kept apart. If someone were kind enough to wash the cups for everyone, his would be set aside; if he were kind enough to wash the cups for others, someone would surely wash those cups again. Things like this reminded him that he had become the easiest person in the room.

38

It was already very dark, and another policeman walks in from outside and says, You haven't left. Xiao Shi tells him that he was on the night shift. The guy says, The chief already said that you don't do the night shift anymore. Xiao Shi asks, Why? The guy says, Don't ask why. Isn't it great not to be on the night shift? He begins to assemble a bed out of chairs while he talks. Xiao Shi says, Why can't I be on the night shift anymore? The guy says, Your wife made a request to the chief (that is, she told the work unit about it). He also says, Isn't it great for a couple to work in the same police station? The wife doesn't have to be on the night shift, and the husband doesn't have to be on the night shift, either. He has the bed half-finished while he talks. The policeman walks over to Xiao Shi and says, Excuse me, I need to use the chair. Then he yanks the chair out from under him. Xiao Shi stands there saying, Why didn't you ask me first? The policeman says, I don't know. Then he says, Isn't it obvious? After a while he (this policeman isn't very happy because he has to work overtime) says, Don't be so ungrateful. Anyhow, you're going to be transferred to another job soon. We've been coworkers for a long time and it's OK that I work a few nights for you. Xiao Shi is surprised again and asks, Where am I going? The policeman says, I don't know. The park police station doesn't suit you anyway. I heard they wanted to assign you to supervise the labor-reform farm. They wanted you to take charge of the men's team. Your wife wouldn't go along with it; but they can't let you take charge of the women's team either. Never mind, enough crap. I don't know anything. From what he said, we understand why homosexuals can't be trusted: you can't use them as men, nor can you use them as women—and you can't use them to supervise men or women.

Xiao Shi locks Ah-Lan's book into his drawer and leaves; he stops when he reaches the gate of the park, not knowing where to go. He doesn't want to go home, but has no place to go if he doesn't return home. Before his eyes lies the night's boundless dark. The despair that surrounded Ah-Lan surrounds him now.